AF392582

WIFEY
TO A
SOUTH CENTRAL
BULLY 2

SHANTAY

Chapter 1

Khalil "Bully" Wright

I replayed Logic's voice in my head over and over. 'Somebody just popped me.' I don't know how the fuck the nigga was able to call me himself. He has strength like a motherfucka. I told him to go to his apartment, and I'd be there with a doctor to check him. Niggas like us have no choice because a hospital was out of the question. Ignoring the fifty billion questions Keyshia threw at me. I had to call Mike and my mama to meet me at Logic's apartment.

"Call my mama and tell her to meet me at Logic's apartment now." I gave her instructions to shut her up. She has been frantic ever since Logic called.

I called Mike on my burner phone. "Wassup?" He answered. I could hear him driving.

"Meet me at Logic's now, bro."

"You good?" He questioned.

"Nigga just got popped."

"Nigga what?" I could hear his tires screech.

I hung up and continued to drive. I made it to the apartment building in fifteen minutes. I parked and ran inside the complex, leaving Keyshia to follow behind me. Running up the stairs, I used my key to unlock his door.

My eyes fell on him, lying on the floor, applying pressure to his wound. This nigga was strong as hell. Immediately I got on the floor to help apply the pressure. Keyshia walked in and screamed, seeing Logic in this state.

"Stop yelling and close the door!" I didn't mean to yell at her, but she couldn't come in and cause a scene. "Go get me a shirt or something!"

She ran to find something for me to use. I pulled out the burner and called Troy, the doctor I've known for years. That nigga was taking his slow ass time when I pay him too much money to handle all my medical needs.

"Nigga where the fuck you at?" I barked into the phone.

"I'm parking now."

"Apartment 307, hurry the fuck up!"

Keyshia returned with a shirt, but Logic looked like he was slipping in and out of consciousness. I told Keyshia to wet a towel to put on his face.

"Keep your eyes open, bro!" I tried my hardest to keep him talking to me. I could see the fear in Logic's eyes, and in my heart, I had it too. I was terrified of losing my brother.

Troy came through the door at the right time. I still hovered over him, watching everything Troy did like I was the operating doctor. He gave Logic some medicine while he pulled out two bullets from his chest. Mike and my mama had come by then. Nobody knew what happened yet, but the second Logic is stable enough to talk I'ma handle it. It took an hour for Troy to remove the bullets and to patch him up.

"One of the bullets was half an inch from his heart," Troy said, wiping off the blood.

Anger spewed deeper inside of me. What nigga was

stupid enough to fuck with Logic? I don't give a fuck if he started some shit with some niggas. They should still fear what could happen to them over his life.

Logic is like the King of all the younger niggas in the city. Everybody and they mama know who he is and who both of his big brothers are. Whenever Logic rolls through places, niggas get up and leave because they know they don't want to be anywhere in sight when shit goes left. Once Troy left, my mama tried to figure out what had happened.

"Not now, mama," I told her. She was getting on my nerves, too, right along with Keyshia.

"Khalil, what do you mean not right now? This boy almost lost his fucking life."

"Mama, can you please take Keyshia home so I can figure this shit out." They were frustrating the fuck out of me.

I get it they both care, and Keyshia has some crazy hormones right now, but the panicking and crying is making me want to shoot my own ears off. I can't even hear myself think right now. Them leaving right now will make the situation a lot smoother and easier for me to find the nigga who did this to him.

"Don't you talk to me like that, Khalil!" She rolled her eyes and got up to leave.

Keyshia looked at me with her tear stained eyes. I motioned for her to come here. "Go home, and get some rest. Call Erin and have her spend the night with you but don't say anything over the phone. I love you, and keep KJ safe for me."

"What if you don't come home?" She cried harder into my chest.

"I promise I'm coming home. Let me handle this,

alright?"

She nodded, but I could tell she wanted to say something. She and my mama left. Now that I got them out of the way, I needed to figure this shit out.

"Now what happened nigga?" Mike asked first.

"He called the burner and said some nigga popped him, and I could hear him groaning in pain. I told him to come here, and I'll meet him here with Troy." That's all I knew.

Mike started to tap Logic's face to wake him. "Get yo' nasty hands off my face nigga." Logic mumbled in agony.

"You could talk now, so what the fuck happened?" I asked him.

"I met up with this girl on the Eastside. We were standing outside her house talking, and a car rolled up and started shooting. I shot back until the nigga drove off. I felt the pain, and that's when I called you."

"What do you remember about the car? Did you see the nigga?" Mike asked.

"Older model blue Toyota and he was light skin. I didn't get to see the full details of his face, but it could have been her baby daddy. He had curly hair. His shit was slick too, like he's mixed or something."

"What makes you think it's her baby daddy?" I asked.

"She said something about her not being from out here and knowing many people. She moved from Las Vegas because her baby daddy would beat on her, and she thinks he's crazy."

"She ain't met crazy yet." Her baby daddy couldn't have been from Los Angeles to fuck with anything attached to Mike and me. For a fact, that nigga didn't know me and know how I step behind anything I love. This nigga will be in a body bag on my dead daughter's soul tonight.

The pain was clear as day on Logic's face, but the pain killers Troy gave him should be kicking in soon. After getting all the information I needed Mike and I left leaving Logic to rest. He wouldn't be of any help in no way, shape, or form, seeing how much pain he is in.

"You got the direct link to the nigga who did it, so don't go spazzing all crazy like you did for April, alright?" Mike calmly said as we walked out of the apartment complex. I don't know what the fuck that was supposed to mean.

"Nigga what? He's your motherfuckin' brother as much as he's mine. You trip on any nigga testing the family." I was ready to square up with him too.

"I agree, but this time you got a wife and a baby on the way to come back home to. You already did time in jail and Keyshia ain't gonna let that shit fly if you get caught up."

He walked off to his truck, leaving me to my thoughts. As much as I thought he was on some weird shit like he was scared or something, he was right. When April passed away, I didn't have anything left. This time I have a family that needs me. That nigga was still going to die, though, and I was going to make it back home to my girl and baby.

I got in my truck and followed behind Mike as we drove to our warehouse on the city's outskirts. This is where we kept our heavy artillery and our lowkey cars for when we needed to ride out. There were machine guns, rifles, revolvers, pistols, and any other kind of gun you could imagine. I started to pick out which gun I wanted to bring. Once they were all loaded, we concealed the weapons in the whip and headed to the location Logic was shot at on the Eastside. I needed to catch this bitch he was talking to because she could be a set up too.

Mike drove as I reclined the seat, thinking about all my next moves. Regardless, Logic is my brother, and there is no way in hell I wouldn't ride out for him. Just because Logic lived this bullet doesn't mean he could live with the next one, and that's my point of why I'm about to show my ass. Nobody should ever touch a hair on that nigga's head.

After about forty-five minutes, we pulled up to the address. The only dim lights came from the faulty streetlights. There was a porch light on, and looking closely, you could see the TV on and shadows in the house.

"Circle the block," I instructed Mike.

When we returned, we could see the same thing. Somebody was in there and was going to give that nigga up. Mike parked a few houses down, leaving the car running. We crept through the gate and walked into the backyard as quietly as possible. Motherfuckas never locked their backdoors. We double checked that we both had gloves and the silencer attached to our guns. Inside, the bitch was sitting in the kitchen with the nigga who shot Logic. Exactly as Logic described the nigga to be, it was him. Both of their eyes shot open when we barged in. The nigga tried to reach for the gun on the table, but I aimed at his hand, shooting him.

"Ahhh!" The bitch screamed.

"You set my brother up bitch?" I forcefully grabbed her by her long hair and held the gun to her head as Mike had his gun set on the nigga who tried to nurse his injured hand.

"I'm sorry, I'm sorry. It wasn't my idea. It was his!" She cried hysterically.

"Bitch I don't give a fuck who idea it was. This became your issue when you inserted yourself."

She tried to run from my firm grip but couldn't. I forcefully snatched her back while ripping some of her hair out. With no emotion, I pulled the trigger to her head, and her body instantly went limp. I dropped her body to the floor before walking over to the nigga. He wanted to be tough. Not wanting to risk beating his ass and getting my DNA all over the kitchen, I pistol-whipped him over and over until his face was unrecognizable. As he curled up into a fetal position, the room was filled with groans.

"You were better off setting up any other nigga." I said before I let my gun riddle bullet holes throughout his body.

"Come on." Mike looked around the room, ensuring we didn't drop or touch anything. We ran out discreetly.

He drove as fast as he could to get out of there, and I hid the guns in the concealed compartments. Once we safely made it to the main streets, he drove normally before getting on the freeway and taking the car to the mechanic. We had already called our nigga Ricky to tell him to stay open late tonight. When we pulled into the parking lot, he was there waiting on our arrival. Mike and I made a lot of smart investments that would cut out any trace of our illegal doings. Ricky worked with us. He and my cousin Jared owned this mechanic shop; whenever niggas needed their whips destroyed, they all came to them. It was a smart ass business. He's going to break this car into pieces and destroy our guns.

"Wassup, my nigga?" I nodded.

"You handled the situation?" He asked.

"Nigga you know I did." Mike and I arrogantly walked to the back office.

Looking out the office window, Ricky had the fire going already, which we were about to use to burn our clothes. We wouldn't ever let anybody do this part for us. We need these clothes burnt to a crisp, especially since I had blood splatter on mine.

Once I watched as the clothes started to burn, I went into the bathroom to wipe off any blood. Looking in the mirror, I felt good knowing I protected my brother, but still, a heavy aura was hovering over me. I don't know what it is, but I had to shake it. That nigga would have doubled back and could have killed any one of us. I looked through the clothes in the closet. I picked a pair of sweatpants, a white t-shirt, and Nike slides to wear. Mike picked the same thing to wear.

"You good?" I asked him. His face was emotionless. Probably still mad from earlier.

"Yeah." I know it was far from the truth.

We walked back outside to see Ricky pulling up with an older model Jeep Cherokee for us. I got in the driver's seat and drove back to the warehouse. In the car, Mike didn't say much. He was always in deep thought, though. We said a few words here and there, but I didn't harass him. When we pulled up to the warehouse, I parked the truck inside, and we left to go to our cars. My car was left at Logic's apartment, so I used one of the lowkey ones I had here.

"I'm about to swing by Logic's place before I go home," I said to Mike.

"I'm a check on him tomorrow." He said. "Be safe,

bro. I'm about to go get Erin from yo' crib."

"Be safe," I said to him.

We both drove off. Once I got on the freeway, I powered back on my cellphone. I always turned it off when I needed to be discreet. I watched as my phone alerted me of all Keyshia's missed calls and texts. I would have called her but decided against it since I still wasn't on my way home yet. I didn't want to promise her I'd be there soon if I knew I wasn't coming right away. It took me twenty minutes to pull up to the raggedy apartment complex. I parked next to Logic's Hellcat. I knocked on the door several times before using my key to enter.

Inside, the place was dark, and there were no noises. I walked into his bedroom, and he was sleeping. I checked to see if he was still breathing. Once he felt me touch him, he jumped up.

"Just me nigga." I said, backing off him.

"The fuck you touching me for?"

"Making sure your ass was still breathing."

It took a minute before he got out of bed to piss. I went into the refrigerator to grab a water bottle. When he came back into the kitchen, he made a bowl of cereal.

"You are about to be twenty-two and live like a ten-year-old. If Mama didn't baby yo' ass, you wouldn't have a choice but to grow up."

"Mama, don't baby shit. She just buys me groceries here and there."

I shook my head because my point exactly.

"Anyways, that bitch set you up."

"No, she didn't." He shook his head.

"You believe I'd lie to you?" I eyed him.

"What happened?" He asked.

"She was in the kitchen giggling and shit with the

same nigga. I've been telling you to keep your eyes open with these bitches. You can't be a wet dick nigga when bitches approach you! Remember who the fuck you are and what these bitches be wanting."

He shook his head in disappointment. One thing about my brother is that he's going to learn his lessons the hard way. I hope he can get his shit together because bitches will be his downfall. When it comes to females, he doesn't have a good judgment of character. He just wanna fuck. He'll raw dog anything.

"I'm a check on you tomorrow. I gotta get home." I told him.

"Alright, be safe." He said, continuing to eat his cereal.

When I got in my truck, the time on the dashboard read 4:24 am. I know Keyshia was having a panic attack since I haven't gotten in touch with her yet, seeing that Erin left by now with Mike. I drove home, passing all the red lights. I couldn't wait to shower and get in bed with my girl anyways. Pulling up to my house, I could see lights were still on. I parked in the garage and went inside, disarming the house alarm. Keyshia came walking down the spiral staircase holding her belly.

"You couldn't pick up your phone?" She had an attitude.

"Nah, I couldn't, babe. I turned it off. I can't be on the phone with you if I'm handling shit." She sighed and walked back into the room. I followed behind her, trying to get her mean ass to stop being mad at me.

"I made it back home safely, and everything is good now, alright? Chill with the attitude, bae."

I went into the bathroom to shower. She didn't follow behind me or protest against it. I let her be. The steaming hot water ran across my body, and I felt the tension release. I don't know how long I was in here, but I just needed a minute to gather my thoughts. Once I was done, I brushed my teeth and dried off. Walking back into the room, Keyshia was tossing and turning on the bed. I could tell she couldn't sleep since she was worried. Quickly I changed in my briefs and grabbed her stretch mark oil on the dresser before sitting beside her. She still had an attitude and didn't want to turn around when I tried to roll her over.

My hands must have felt good all over her body because she dropped the attitude. I haven't missed one night rubbing her body down with oil. Knowing her brat ass, she probably was mad thinking I wouldn't come home to oil her.

"Are you going to tell me the real reason why you're mad?" I asked.

"I was scared. It didn't make it any better you didn't answer my phone calls. You always answer my phone calls no matter what you're doing."

"You are right, but not this time, bae. I had shit to handle. If I would have been answering you and doing what you wanted me to do, I could have fucked up. I executed that shit carefully and can't have anything firing back at Mike and me, alright?"

"Listen, I know you were in the streets from when I first met you and still chose to pursue a relationship with you. Then we ended up getting pregnant, and things changed. I cannot lose you, Khalil. I love you more than I love my fucking self. I need you! You are all I have left."

"Nothing is going to happen to me." The waterworks started to fall from her eyes. "Don't cry, bae."

"I was so scared you wouldn't come back home."

She cried hysterically.

"Every time I leave this house, I promise I will make it back home to you and KJ. You don't need to ever worry. When it comes to you, my family, and my money, I do whatever I have to do to protect us."

"How is Logic? I wanted to call and check on him, but I know you would disapprove of it." She wiped away her tears.

"He's alright. You can go check on him tomorrow."

"This has been a crazy night." She got comfortable before drifting off to sleep.

Rubbing her belly, I felt KJ move. I smiled knowing my son felt my presence. It felt good as fuck to be back home and safely in bed with my wife. I watched Keyshia sleep, but my mind was on overdrive. Before I knew it the sun was rising, and I still had trouble sleeping.

I got up from the bed and changed into my sweats and a long sleeve before slipping on my Nike's and going into the backyard. I needed to work out to clear my mind and tire my body. I lay on the bench and lifted the weights. Working out keeps me on my toes and my fist hard as iron.

Chapter 2

Keyshia Wright

I promise you my life is not meant to have any peace or happiness. When things start to go good, bad always follows. First, Granny passed away, and I'm just now beginning to see the sunlight and smile again. Then here goes Logic getting shot. If all of that wasn't enough to deal with, KJ has been kicking my ass during this pregnancy.

Christmas is a couple of weeks away, and truly in my heart, I want to say fuck everything. I want to continue to grieve over Granny, but I cannot sulk into my depression forever. KJ's health depended on me keeping my mind strong. I'm doing everything I can to stay busy since Bully isn't always at home to keep me positive.

"Who's at the door?" Bully asked, entering the kitchen.

"The Christmas tree delivery." I followed behind him to answer the door.

Since this is our first Christmas as a family, I decided on a grand tree. We have such a beautiful house, so why not be extra with the decorations? I instructed the delivery guys where I wanted the tree. I had a unique ornament of my mommy and Granny's face I will be placing on the tree. Even though they aren't here anymore, they're here in spirit.

"That's a big ass tree." Bully looked at the tree that towered over him.

"That's the point."

"Who's going to decorate it?" He asked.

"I have a tree decorator that's going to come by."

"You just be making shit up at this point." He shrugged.

"You'll see once it gets done."

"You know what you want for Christmas?" He asked.

"I wish I could have Granny back." He opened his arm for a hug. I melted in his embrace.

"I know." He kissed my forehead.

"What do you have planned for today?" I asked him.

"Gotta check on a couple of stuff, then I'm going to the club to get things together with Pamela. We're getting closer and closer to the grand opening, and I need to stay focused right now. What are you doing today?"

We ended up hiring the thirsty bitch Pamela as the manager. Even though she tried it with me, she had excellent references and knew what she was doing. I'm not jealous by a long shot, and I made it very clear to keep shit professional in here 'cause she wouldn't make it out of the club without a busted eye and a broken jaw.

"Oh, good. Nothing. I am going to go shopping for presents."

"Call me when you're done later, and we can go out for dinner." He kissed my lips and then KJ before he left.

I went upstairs to go shower and get dressed. When the water hit my body, I scrubbed thoroughly and quickly got out. I went into my closet and looked for the perfect outfit to wear. I picked a brown off-the-shoulder floor-length dress. It hugged my body, and my baby bump looked so cute. After I moisturized, I changed into the dress before doing my hair and applying light makeup. I stopped to take pictures in the mirror before I left to send them to Bully.

Once in my car, I blasted my music and drove to Neiman Marcus. I couldn't wait for my shopping spree. The thought of it all was burning a hole through my wallet. As I drove, my phone rang. I answered quickly, seeing that it was Erin.

"Hi, boo." I gleamed when I answered.

"Hey, bitch. I miss you!"

"I miss you too."

"Where are you going? I can hear you driving."

"Christmas shopping."

"I already know how that is going to go." She sighed.

"What do you mean?" I giggled.

"You are about to be in these stores until they close, and you'll resume tomorrow when they open again. You don't play when Christmas comes around."

"You don't complain when opening your gifts, though."

"I sure as hell don't. I don't have another friend that gifts Chanel bags." We both laughed. "Are you coming to the club?" She asked.

"I didn't have any plans on it. Did Pamela call you in?" I asked.

Erin agreed to work at the club. She'd be in charge of the bottle service girls and ensuring everything runs as it should. It comes with great pay and all tips, plus I'm sure she's happy she didn't have to deal with these niggas anymore.

"Yeah, she said it's a meeting with everyone."

"Bully will be there. I don't feel like coming in. I don't feel like dealing with people today."

"I understand."

"I'ma call you later. I'm pulling up to valet right now."

"Alright." She hung up.

"Welcome to Neiman Marcus." The valet attendant opened my car door for me.

I grabbed my Bottega Venetta bag off the passenger seat and took the ticket he gave me before walking inside. I walked over to the shoe department and began picking out heels and sandals. There were a lot of cute items on display that I hadn't seen before.

"I'll take this one too." I handed the shopper a Gucci slipper.

I paid and then headed upstairs to see what I could get Bully. My man is just as fly as me, and I know everything he has in his closet. He loved to dress, and he damn sure looked good when he stepped out. I walked over to the shoe department and looked for something new. As I browsed the shoe selection, I heard my name being called.

"I knew it was you." I turned to see Raheem standing in my face. He leaned in for a hug, but I stopped him. This man could never leave me alone. His eyes roamed my body, landing on my baby bump. "You're pregnant?" He looked at me in disgust.

"And married?" I waved my beautiful wedding ring. He was getting ready to say something, but I stopped him. "Listen, Raheem. I don't want to speak to you. It's not one reason why we need to speak. I don't want a friendship, and it's not cordial when we see each other. You know how loyal I am when I'm in a relationship. My man sure wouldn't appreciate you talking to me, especially since you work for him, Raheem."

I don't know if Raheem meant any harm or not, but I'm not allowing any room for an ex to think he could feel superior to my husband. My man isn't insecure but will go to war over me. I'm trying to spare this guy, but his emotions won't allow him to see that. I don't want the friendship, especially since this is the second time running into him since I've been with Bully. I'm sure I'd see him here and there, but I don't give a fuck about being cordial. Bully doesn't play about me, and I'm sure Raheem knows that.

"You let that nigga put a baby in you?" He frowned.

"Like how you cheated on me and put babies in other women? Raheem, you gotta back up. I'm not even tryna tell Bully you're coming at me like this because it won't end well for you. Just keep making your money over there and ignore me 'cause I'm ignoring you. You have better shit to worry about than what I'm doing with my husband." I walked off.

"Does your Granny know what this nigga do? I'm tryna tell you Keyshia he ain't the one for you!" He followed behind me, trying to get me to listen.

"Don't let my Granny's name come out of your mouth. You don't give a fuck about her or me, in all honestly. Your pride just won't let you see me with a better than you in your face. It's quite funny, actually. Granny loves Bully, and not that it's any of your business, she passed away."

His mouth dropped. I walked away, but this time

for good. I was sick of this nigga. There was no way I would let him continue speaking to me. Bully had spies everywhere, and I wasn't trying to let the wrong story get back to him. We have trust, and I would never do anything weird to break our bond. I browsed the clothes selection, picking up a few things for my man before heading to the baby department. I wanted to see if there was anything new I could buy KJ. My shopping trip ended three hours later. I couldn't hold these bags anymore. They started to get too heavy. Once the valet pulled my truck up, I called Bully immediately.

"Hey, babe," I said when he answered.

"Wassup, baby mama?" I blushed. He sounded like he was still busy.

"I'm ready to eat."

"Come to the club. Chef is here, and I'll have him cook us up something if you cool with that."

"Sounds like a plan to me."

"Call me when you get outside so I can come to get you."

"Alright, babe."

I hung up and headed to the club. I couldn't wait for this meal. My mouth salivated, thinking about the food I'd devour soon. The drive took about twenty minutes. I pulled into the parking lot and parked next to Mike's Escalade. I called Bully for him to escort me inside as he promised. It took less than two minutes for him to come outside. My heart smiled, seeing his sexy ass walking towards me to open the car door.

"You look good as fuck." He squeezed my ass.

"Yes, hype me up! Tryna do whatever to look good for my man." I flirted.

"You always look beautiful, mama." He kissed my

lips.

"Thank you, babe."

I held on to his hand as we walked into the club. There were a lot of people here today. Seeing everything come together made me so excited for Bully. He has put so much time and energy into getting this nightclub open. There has been a complete three-sixty change since he first started. *Club Empire* is more for the elite crowd. I greeted everyone as we walked into the kitchen, where Chef was preparing our meal.

"Everything smells amazing, Chef." I looked over him, sautéing garlic in a pan.

"Can't wait for you to try some new menu items, Mrs. Wright."

"I can't wait either!"

I walked off with Bully into his office. Once we went inside, he couldn't keep his hands off me. The warmth from his touches and his soft kisses on my neck sent chills to my spine. He lifted my dress and slid my thong to the side before bending me over the desk. Being five and a half months pregnant didn't stop anything. Quickly I turned over, touching my toes, not needing the desk for balance. Slowly he slid his dick inside, and I helped by bouncing my ass to help guide him.

I thought I wouldn't have a sex drive while being pregnant, but I was hornier than before. If I felt any nausea fucking made it go away. It was so weird, but I'm grateful 'cause I worried our sex life would die. I needed dick morning, noon, and night.

"Fuckkk. You so tight, ma." He whispered.

I tried my hardest to keep my moans low as possible, but anybody walking by could hear us. My pussy was soaking wet. It just made him go harder until he climaxed in me.

"Damn!" I tried to catch my breath.

It was a quickie but intense. I forgot I came here to eat. Now I just wanna go home to go to sleep. He helped me walk to the bathroom because my legs felt like noodles. I could hardly stand up on my own. I cleaned myself up while he did the same.

"Yo' pussy been extra creamy since you've been pregnant." He said as he finished cleaning himself off.

Before I could respond, I heard a knocking at the door. He washed his hands off before going to answer it. I continued to clean myself off properly before walking back inside. Pamela was going over some paperwork. Her facial expression changed when I entered. I promise you I wanna fuck this hoe up, but for the business, I'ma chill.

"You see my girl. Speak!" Bully caught the same thing I did. Glad it wasn't just me tripping as usual.

"Oh, yeah, hi Keyshia."

"Mrs. Wright." I fake smiled. This bitch was never a friend of mine to call me by my first name.

I sat on the sofa and watched her mannerisms. She was nervous when I came around, but she paid attention to me. I could see her ass staring on the low. That's how I know this bitch is still tryna be sneaky. The second this bitch oversteps, I'm personally dragging her out pregnant or not, and Bully could just be mad at me later.

"Alright, what are you waiting around for?" Bully caught an attitude with her. She acted as if he invited her to come in here and kick it with us.

"Sorry." She ran to the door.

"Aye, wait." He said, and she stopped in her tracks.

"I could have sworn I checked yo' ass earlier. I don't want nothing you are offering bitch, and when you see my wife, you give her all of your respect. Do your job and only that when you enter my shit." Authority laced his voice. He made me straighten up, and I didn't even do shit.

"Y-yes." She nodded and then walked out.

"Dumb ass bitch." I co-signed like he asked for my opinion.

"You late as hell with your reply. She gone already, bae. You want me to tell her to come back?" He chuckled, and I couldn't stop laughing. "So, is there still any money left on my card after your shopping trip?" he asked.

"Boy, stop playing with me. I can buy a jet today, and there will still be money on that card." I giggled. A smile spread across his face 'cause he knew I was telling the truth. Money wasn't a problem to Bully. The way money flows to him, you would think there's a money tree in our backyard.

"Y'all done fucking?" Erin knocked on the door. This bitch has no filter and lets anything come out of her mouth. I couldn't stop laughing. I got up to answer the door.

"You don't miss anything, do you?" I asked when I opened the door.

"Girl, everybody up here could hear, *oh Khalil fuck me harder.*" She mimicked what I was saying during our quickie.

"Y'all need to mind y'all business." I rolled my eyes.

"We were, but Chef was done with y'all food, and I helped him bring it up for you."

She went back outside to push in the rolling table of food. "So, what are we eating?"

"Where is your man Erin?" I asked seconds before Mike walked in.

"He don't be feeding me like Bully feeds you."

"Don't sit up here and lie to them. What the fuck is wrong with you?" Mike came over and greeted me.

The four of us had a close family bond. Our double dates are funny as hell, and I think we all look forward to it each time. Erin was like a little sister to Bully, and I loved that he accepted all of her craziness like I did. He didn't judge her and looked out for her whether I was around or not. Mike and I had a similar relationship. I loved having him around. He was so chill, and he looked out for Bully. I know my man is safe whenever he's with Mike and vice versa.

"Don't nobody believe her ass," Bully said, taking an envelope of money from Mike and stashing it away.

"We about to get out of here," Mike said, dragging Erin's nosey ass out of the office.

"Now everybody knows we were in here fucking." I said to Bully.

"We are grown and own this shit. They'll be alright." He never gave a fuck about anything.

He wheeled the table to the sofa so we could sit and enjoy our meal. Chef made stuffed salmon, garlic butter shrimp, mashed potatoes, and asparagus. Everything smelled delicious. We said our grace and devoured our meal.

"This is so good, babe!" The salmon melted in my mouth.

"It is good." He tore it up too.

"I was thinking about what you said last night during my shopping trip."

"What are you talking about?" He looked confused.

"About us going on a honeymoon soon."

"Oh, so now you want to go?" He sighed.

"Yes, I was thinking Jamaica or a cruise."

"Alright, set it up. It'll be nice to get away for a few days."

I couldn't hide the excitement on my face. Thinking about how relaxing it would be to have a honeymoon on an island, or a cruise made me excited as fuck. With all that is going on in my mind and heart, I could use the getaway. It would be an excellent time for me to focus on our marriage so we could enjoy the alone time we have left. Once KJ gets here, it's over for our privacy.

Chapter 3

Michael "Mike" Simmons

I looked at my GPS, directing me to a family-style home in Torrance with a big For Rent sign on the yard. The 2,500-square-foot home could be the start of Erin and me taking our relationship to the next level. We've been together for over a year, and everything about this woman drives me crazy, but something isn't right between us. I watched her eyes roam the gated house. I couldn't read her like I usually could. I got out of the truck and opened the door for her. We walked inside the open house.

I would do anything to make us a family. The only reason why I would rent and not buy a house with her is because I don't know where this relationship is going. I want us to get on the same page and see her let her walls down. I know she's been through a lot, so I'm trying not to push too hard, but it's hard as fuck not to. I'm just not understanding why she's so hesitant.

"You like it?" I asked as we walked through the house.

"It's stunning and spacious."

The four-bedroom, three-bathroom home could fit both of us and my daughter comfortably with room for a baby. I'm in this relationship all the way. I see myself making Erin my wife, but I honestly don't know where I stand with her. I know she loves me for sure, and that's the only reason I'm sticking around. We're still distant in parts of our relationship. She says she's guarding her heart. If we can't come to common grounds, I'll bow out gracefully because, at this point, it feels like I'm chasing someone who isn't interested sometimes.

"Should we apply?" I stared into her eyes, already sensing her answer.

"I don't know if I'm ready, Mike." Exactly like I thought she would say.

"Ready for what, Erin? I'm with you twenty-four-seven, pay your bills, take care of you and everything else, but putting our name on a lease is where you draw the line?" I backed up when she tried to touch me.

"It's not like that!" She whined.

"Then what is it like?"

She didn't say anything, and that's all I needed to hear. "Come on."

I couldn't reason with her anymore. We walked out of the house, and I opened the car door for her. Once I got in my truck, I headed straight to her condo. We were supposed to chill today since we haven't been on a date in weeks. She had already started school and was busy day and night. I wanted this for her as much as she wanted it for herself. I've been supporting her dreams and not complaining.

We didn't speak the whole car ride. It wasn't anything to say. I pulled up to the apartment complex and unlocked the doors. She looked at me with so much hurt in her eyes. She didn't expect me to drop her off and not come inside with her. I needed my space. Maybe it isn't a good idea for us to live together.

"You not coming in?" She turned to face me.

"Nah."

She got out of the car but still stood there waiting. I couldn't deal with her ass, so I drove off. This girl has a big place in my heart, and it pissed me off more that I was treating her bad for her icing me out like this. I shook my head and headed to the gas station. Erin don't gotta worry about me. She could give the sob stories to the next nigga.

I parked my truck next to Bully's. He was standing outside talking with the niggas guarding the gas station. Getting out of the car, I walked over there and dapped them all up.

"I thought you were with your girl?" Bully asked.

I just shook my head and left it at that. Logic walked out of the gas station, eating a burger. He was back on his feet and good as new. Since then, Bully and I had to get on his head about the immature shit he's been doing. The bullet pumped fear in his ass because he straightened up quickly.

"There's food in the office." Logic said.

I nodded my head and went in there to grab a burger too. I was hungry as fuck since we didn't make it to dinner like we had planned. Bully came in with me since it was only Bully, Logic, and I allowed back here.

"What happened?" Bully asked, pulling a chair up to the table.

"I'm done doing this back and forth with Erin. She plays too many games. I'm not about to keep chasing behind a female that acts like she doesn't want me."

"She still doing that shit?" He sounded frustrated along with me.

"We went to the rental property, and it was the

same shit. I dropped her off home and dipped. I can't keep wasting my time."

"You think she got another nigga or something?" He asked.

"Nah, she's just broken as fuck, and I can't help someone who doesn't want to be healed." I threw a couple of fries in my mouth.

"I was about to go home, and they're about to roll up to the strip club." He referred to Logic and some of the niggas from the team.

"I'm in. Ain't shit else to do." I nodded my head.

We ate the burgers and fries before parting ways. Bully went home, and Logic rode with me to the strip club. We were meeting our niggas there. Making it to Hollywood, I parked in the parking lot, opting out of valet. Before going in, we stayed in the truck and passed the blunt back and forth.

"You been good lil' bro?" I asked Logic.

"You know how I do." He cockily chuckled.

"I hope you have been staying away from these bitches."

"Not staying away but moving smarter."

"I guess that's a step up from what you were doing."

Bully and Logic were my real family. I didn't have any siblings, so we stayed close. My mom was close to them and vice versa. My daughter only knew them as her uncles, and that's how it has always been. Once we finished off the blunt, all the homies arrived. We got out of the truck and went inside.

"Be careful and pay attention," I told Logic seeing his eyes were filled with lust.

I'ma always protect him regardless. As soon as we got into our section, the bitches ran to come in here. Whenever we stepped out, we always got the royal treatment. But money hungry bitches would do that too. There was some Instagram model here hosting the club tonight, and it was crowded. *Ginuwine Pony* played loud throughout the club. The strippers in our section were putting in overtime. The club was packed from wall to wall. I was starting to feel like I couldn't breathe for a minute. Monday nights were always the most packed.

My eyes locked with a dancer that I've never seen here before. She must've been new 'cause I'd for sure remember her ass. She shook her ass while cuffing her ankles tightly. I watched as her cheeks moved like a tidal wave. She walked off the stage and came into my section, searching for me. When she sat on my lap, I didn't object to it.

Her heels made her tall, so I couldn't estimate her actual height, but she was sexy as fuck. Her chocolate skin was glowing, and her body was perfect from head to toe. Nothing looked out of place on her. She whined her waist on me.

"How come I haven't seen you here before?" She whispered in my ear before rubbing her hands across my body.

"I was wondering the same thing," I smirked.

She smiled before continuing her lap dance. All the homies in my section were on her, but we stayed focused on each other. She was on my dick, and I didn't mind at all. I'm done chasing behind Erin, so I didn't mind her company.

"Nigga what about Erin?" Logic pulled my arm and asked.

I shrugged. "We not fucking with each other."

I focused my attention back on the fun I was

having. For some reason, I felt so relaxed. My guard was still up since I always kept my eyes open and paid attention. I drank a bottle of Ace to myself and smoked my blunt, enjoying the scene.

We didn't leave the club until after three in the morning. I dropped Logic off at his apartment and headed straight home. I had to be up early to pick Kiki up for my weekend with her. Her little ass would trip if I wasn't on time. If not, I would have stayed a little longer at the strip club.

When I made it home, I took off my clothes to lay in bed until I fell asleep. I was high and needed some sleep. I woke up to the sound of my phone going off. I immediately jumped up because it was the ringtone for my daughter. As soon as I answered, I knew I was late to pick her up, and it would be yet another problem with her mama.

"Hey, baby," I answered.

"Daddy, where are you?" She sounded sad.

"Sorry, baby, I'm just now waking up. I'm about to get in the shower, and I'll make it up to you."

"Hurry up. I wanna leave."

"You alright?" I asked.

"Yeah, mama, just yelling because you're late."

"Alright, I'ma hurry up."

I hung up the phone and rushed to shower as I promised. My baby girl meant the whole world to me, and I didn't mean to upset her. She was a daddy's girl, so me not being on time had her tripping. I wasn't even in the shower fifteen minutes before I rushed out. Quickly I dried off and grabbed some clothes from my closet. I chose a pair of Chrome Hearts jeans and the matching long sleeve shirt to wear. I pulled my dreads back and sprayed on my cologne. I searched for my keys because I didn't know where I had left them. Since I couldn't find it, I pulled out the Lamborghini for Kiki. It was her favorite car.

It took me fifteen minutes to get to my baby mama's house. I moved her to the quieter part of Los Angeles. Shana was a fling until I got her pregnant. I was young and felt like the man in the streets. I was doing so much reckless shit I had no business doing, including fucking Shana raw. I understood why Logic moved the way he did. Being a young nigga from the streets with so much power and money, you felt unstoppable.

Once I found out she was pregnant, I officially tried to make the relationship work. I wasn't a dead-beat nigga, and I knew Shana wasn't just fucking everybody, so I stepped up. Once she gave birth to Kiki, I got a DNA test even though I didn't need to. From the second I took my first glance at my baby girl, I knew she was mine. She looked exactly like me and not a trace of her mama. Physically I was attracted to Shana. That's why I was fucking her so deep, but mentally I didn't care for her in that way. I broke it off because it was getting too toxic. She was in her feelings, but I had already expected that. Since then, I still managed to find a way to co-parent with her. She made that shit hard as hell, though. I know she was jealous I was giving my time to Erin. I sighed before stepping out of my car. I didn't feel like seeing her, but I had no choice. I walked to the door and knocked, waiting for her to answer it.

"Hi, daddy!" Kiki beamed before rushing to hug me.

"Wassup Kiki? Go get your stuff so we can go." She ran upstairs to grab her purse. She never left without one. She was a grown woman in a seven-year-old body, I swear.

She was sassy as fuck like her mama but a tomboy inside.

"Finally! What took you so long?" Shana walked into the foyer where I stood.

"I don't think that's your business. Plus, you're always late when you pick her up." She rolled her eyes like I knew she would. I could see her peeking out the door to see if Erin was in the car. "Don't break your neck trying to be nosey."

"Boy, don't nobody give a fuck about what you have going on." She rolled her eyes again and yelled for Kiki to hurry up.

"I'm coming." Kiki ran down the stairs with her Gucci sunglasses, purse, and phone in her hand.

"You a grown ass woman Kiki." I chuckled before escorting her to the car.

"Oh, we're about to have fun today, daddy." She said, seeing the Lamborghini parked outside.

I opened the door for her, and she got inside. I took her to the mall and let her ball out like she usually does. My daughter won't be in any necessary heartbreak when she gets older. I'm laying out the red carpet for her now, so she knows how to be treated and what won't be tolerated. I'd lay my life down to ensure my children have the best of everything, and I stand on that.

"You excited about your birthday party?" I asked her.

Her party is next weekend, and we're throwing it at Sky Zone. She was adamant it had to be a glow-in-the-dark party, and whatever she wanted, she could have. I paid to have the place shut down for her and all of her friends. We are going to do it up big for her because she deserves it.

"I am so excited!" She smiled ear to ear. "Mama

showed me what my cake will look like."

"I'm glad you're excited. Are all of your friends coming?"

"Yes, and people at my school I don't even talk to wanna come." She said with an attitude.

I chuckled because Kiki is a handful. We pulled up to the mall, and I opened the door for her to get out. She threw on her sunglasses, and I followed her bossy ass around. Kiki knows whenever she's with her daddy; she can have whatever she wants. Her mama started to let her dress herself since she was getting older, and she swears now she's a fashion designer since she can put her clothes together. I see that in her future because she does love fashion. That's what she and Erin bonded over. Whenever it was my weekend, she would play in Erin's closet, and Erin would take her to the mall with her, and they would match outfits together.

"I wish Erin was here." She said, searching through a rack of clothes.

"Yo' daddy ain't fun to hang with?" I felt offended.

"It's not that, daddy. We just have fun together picking out clothes."

"No, y'all just like spending my money."

"I do." She giggled.

I ain't gon' lie. That shit made me sad inside, knowing she wanted to be with Erin. It made me mad as fuck at her that she couldn't get her shit together. We already took all the steps to be a family just for her to act weird as fuck in the end. I don't know what the future will look like for us, but for now, we gotta go our separate ways. It was getting toxic, and she didn't even see it.

Kiki called Erin on FaceTime to help her with an outfit. Her mama was taking her and some of her friends out to the movies after school in a couple of days, so she wanted to be fly. I could dress and throw shit together, but she had this special bond that only Erin could fill. I don't even hear her talking about her mama when it comes to dressing. I fell back and carried her shopping bags while she showed Erin every outfit she thought was cute to her.

Chapter 4

Erin Jackson

Days have gone by, and I still haven't heard from Mike. I've been blowing up his phone and he refuses to answer. I don't want us to break up, but if we are, I don't want it to be like this. I'm just mad as fuck that he can't find the courage to say how he feels. I tried to get my mind off the situation and focus on my test. I've been studying for this exam for the past week. I've managed to keep my grades up and focus on the opening of Club Empire. It was a lot of work, but it's all worth it.

I finished my test and turned it in before class was over. As I walked to my car my phone rang, and it was Mike. I quickly answered because there was no way I would let him slide with this bullshit.

"Hello," I answered.

"Wassup?"

"You tell me, Mike."

"You out of class yet?" He asked.

"Yeah, just got out."

"You got time to meet me?" I don't know why he sounded like a setup. He usually doesn't talk like this. He sounded like he was done, and it scared me. I could hear it in his voice.

"Yeah, where at?"

"I'll send you the address. It's by your school."

"Okay."

He hung up and sent the address. I typed it in my GPS, and he was six minutes away. Before I drove off, I got myself together. I fluffed my hair and slicked my baby hair down with the edge control and brush in my purse. I sprayed on my Baccarat A La Rose and applied lip gloss before driving off. My stomach was in knots. I didn't know what to expect, but it felt like he would tell me he was breaking it off with me.

It was a cafe, and he was seated outside at one of the tables. I parked at the meter and walked across the street. When I approached him, he half smiled and didn't hug me. That was the first red flag. I still sat down across from him.

"You look good." He said vaguely.

"You do too." I couldn't deny it. He was so sexy to me.

He reached into his pocket and handed me the key to my apartment. "I cleared my things out and wanted to see you face to face. At first, I wasn't, but I'm a man, and I'm not gonna trip out on you like a hoe."

"Are you serious right now?" Instantly my heart got to pumping, and tears filled my eyes.

"I'm dead serious right now, E. I love you but you gotta heal first. You let people break you down so bad that you started to break me down. I want the best for you, ma, but you're not what's best for me at this moment."

I cried hearing him say this. I felt like he could have held on longer. I wasn't out here cheating on him or making him look bad. I was just taking baby steps. What more does he expect from me?

"Why did you bring me here for this? Why couldn't you tell me this at home?"

"In no way, shape or form do I want you to feel like I'm ganging up on you or about to hurt you. I'm still tryna be light on you despite how I feel. You have been so delicate, and I can't keep wondering if I'm saying or doing the right thing when it comes to your trauma. As I said, you are a dope ass person, but you have to heal E. You can't keep bleeding on the people that love you the most."

I didn't say anything; I just cried because I couldn't believe this. He looked like he wanted to cry his damn self, so why would he leave me like this? If this is hurting him too, we should be able to fix it together than be separated.

"I moved all your stuff back into the apartment. Kiki's birthday party is this weekend; if you still want to be there, you are welcome. It doesn't have to be weird, and you don't have to worry about Shana. You know Kiki loves you, and I'm not being spiteful towards you. I love you, E."

He bent down and kissed my forehead before walking off. I couldn't believe this shit. I got up, walked to my car across the street, and called Keyshia.

"Are you okay?" She answered, hearing me balling crying.

"He broke up with me!" My heart felt empty.

"Are you serious? I thought he was just cooling down."

"I thought so too! He called me to meet him at a cafe by my school, and he gave me back my key, moved all my stuff back in, and took his stuff."

"Damn." Keyshia couldn't even say anything. "What did he say? What was his reasoning?"

"He says I need to heal because now I'm hurting him. I don't want him to leave me, Keyshia." I cried even harder. I love this man, but how he put it felt like he was with me out of guilt.

"You wanna come over or want me to meet you at home?" She asked.

"No. I have to breathe."

"I promise you it's going to be okay, Erin. Take some time to breathe. He probably just needs space, and you do too to sort through these emotions."

"Yeah." I dryly said before hanging up.

He was done with me for sure. He was completely done with the look in his eyes and the hurt that laced his voice. I always seemed to self-destruct somehow. Once I got myself together somewhat, I drove home. I just wanted to shower and crawl under a rock. As I drove, I silently cried, not knowing how I didn't see this coming. I parked in my parking spot and rushed inside. In the living room were three black trash bags of everything I had at his house. I cried more, realizing this shit was happening right now. I went straight to my closet, and it was half empty. He removed every single thing leaving all the stuff he bought me. He didn't take anything back. All my bags and jewelry were still there.

I went to grab my phone to call him, but he didn't answer. He was really serious about this breakup. I gave up trying to plead my case. I didn't have any more fight left in me. I got up to get in the shower to wash away my day. I couldn't let this break me, but it damn sure hurts. I felt like I'm internally bleeding from this heartache. I have never loved anyone like this before, not even Edward. I don't know how I'm supposed to shake him from my heart and mind.

In the shower, I tried my hardest to rid Mike of my thoughts to feel better, but all I could think about was the memories we shared. That man made me so happy, and I finally felt love for the first time. My life didn't feel so dark anymore because he was my light. I didn't know the whole time I thought I was healing I was hurting him. We never had this conversation before, so I don't understand why he can't just hear me out. Yes, I've been trying to put it off for months when it comes to living under one roof. Living together scares me. I feel like we'll jinx this amazing love once we make it official and move in together. He doesn't see that I'm trying to protect our love.

On the other hand, I'm questioning what I ever meant to him. How could he pick up and leave so easily? How could we go from speaking all day to never speaking again? Keyshia had sent me a screen recording from Logic's Instagram story the day Mike and I got into our argument. He went to the strip club, and his face was buried in one of the stripper's asses. My heart shattered into pieces when I saw the video. It's like he was purposely trying to hurt me. I have no doubt in my mind that he fucked one of them bitches. The look he had in his eyes was the same when he stared at me.

Now here I am contemplating whether I am good enough. I promised myself no man would make me spiral again like Edward did. I almost kissed my life goodbye when I caught him cheating on me. Even though I am telling myself that Mike is not worth any of these emotions, I know I cannot keep lying to myself. I love this man with my whole being. Other than this misunderstanding, we had something special. I was able to experience love with this man, so I'm not okay.

I got out of the shower and dried myself off before applying lotion. I just wanted to lay in bed and cry. This is the worse heartbreak ever. I felt like I had lost a happy part of me, which irked my soul. Looking in my drawer, I found a crop top and a pair of shorts to wear.

My bedroom felt like it was spinning, and I needed to sit down. The whole condo felt empty and cold. I continued to check my phone to see if he would call me back, but there was nothing. My thoughts were speaking loud, and I couldn't keep doing this to myself. I got up and unpacked all of the things he brought over. I felt sad putting everything away but had to keep my mind busy.

When I was done, I turned on my music and pulled out my school bag to get some homework done. In the midst of it, I continued to feel myself about to lose my shit. Nothing was keeping me focused. I have been through too much in my life and came out on top every time. Shouldn't this situation be any different, right?

I opened my laptop and searched for a new therapist. My old therapist didn't help me the way I felt like I needed help. He just kept prescribing me pills, and that shit made me crazier. I needed someone to hear me out and help me sort through these emotions and trauma I was dealing with. It took me an hour to find Doctor Shonda. She's an African American woman, and her reviews were all from people who were broken and needed healing. I called to set up my first appointment.

"Hi, I want to schedule a session with Doctor Shonda," I spoke when the receptionist answered.

She took my information and said Doctor Shonda had one opening today before closing, and I took it immediately. I needed it more today than ever. The appointment was in an hour, so I quickly got dressed and made my way to her office, which was twenty minutes away from my apartment.

I don't know why I felt so good as I drove. For some reason, I felt like I would finally be heard. My heart and mind is so fucked up, honestly. I don't know what love is and never felt it before, Mike. The only thing that felt somewhat healthy in my life is him, and that's why I'm having such a hard time accepting this.

I parked in the parking lot and made it ten minutes before my appointment. I rushed inside, ready for help. I signed in and paid for my session before sitting in the waiting area waiting for her.

"Ms. Jackson, nice to meet you." Doctor Shonda exited her office to greet me. She is a beautiful mid-age woman.

"Nice to meet you, Doctor Shonda."

I followed behind her and took a seat on the couch. Her office was very plush. She sat down in her chair and got comfortable before introducing herself, and I spoke about the few things that have occurred in my life.

"Do you feel at fault for your father's death?" She asked after I gave her the cliff note version of my chaotic life.

"I do, but I don't feel sorry for him. I'm happy actually that someone murdered him in there."

Every emotion from my childhood resurfaced. I remember when my social worker came to my elementary school and broke the news. I went back to my foster home happy that day. I felt safe knowing he couldn't get to me again. He molested me for months and months. He didn't care about me being his daughter, and I don't care about him either.

"So, how is the relationship with your mom in present day?" She asked.

"We don't have a relationship. I have not seen her

since she gave me away. My egg donor called me every liar in the book when I told her what my sperm donor was doing to me. That's why I told my teacher so somebody could finally believe me."

"Do you feel like you had physically grown and turned into this beautiful woman over the years but mentally and emotionally, you are still stuck at age seven when you were being abused?" She asked.

"Yes." I silently cried.

"Sometimes we get hurt, and we stop growing. We can be forty years old with a mind of a seven-year-old because that's where our brain is still stuck at. Trauma often keeps us swimming in the pain like a bad dream you can't wake up from. That's why it's important to sort through these emotions and thrive so you can form safe relationships with yourself and other people."

"All of my life, I felt unhappy. I would see my mom cater to this man and not care about me. She would cook dinner, feed him, and leave me starving until he said it was okay for me to eat. Then I remember him drinking more and more. It turned our household upside down. He would beat her up until she was purple in the face. My mom never cared. Now that I am older, I think she had a mental problem. I would come home from school and play, trying to tune out the noise of him beating her to a bloody pulp. Then that's when he started to molest me. I don't feel like going into details about that part, but it happened, and it damaged me to this very day." I sobbed hysterically.

"What makes you think it damaged you?"

"I don't know how to love freely. Every time I get close to somebody, I guard my heart before they can hurt me. In high school, I was so lost. I didn't have sex with every guy I met, but I fiend for their attention. They thought I was pretty, and I wanted to be accepted and feel wanted. It doesn't matter who the person is I need to please them, and it doesn't matter to what extent. I seriously hate I'm a people pleaser. Then I met Edward. Now that we aren't together, I think back to how I morphed into my parents in that relationship. I was attentive and dismissive at the same time as my mom. Then at times, a narcissist like my dad.

Edward is a piece of shit. At first, he was the perfect guy. He treated me pretty well, but then he went to jail. He did some time, and I decided to stay with him. I felt like I needed to be by his side. I didn't see myself interpreting my mom in the relationship then. I became super submissive, and he became mentally abusive. He never laid hands on me but manipulated me every chance he got. I would pay all the bills, take care of the home, fuck him, and feed him. I even bought him a car and all of the designer clothes he asked for. He wanted to be treated like a king, and I did that. There was nothing I wouldn't do for him. I was busting my ass to make him happy while he did nothing to contribute to our relationship. He was cheating on me the whole time, and I was still willing to make it work. I come home one day, and he is in my bed with his friend and a woman having a threesome. I've had enough trauma at that point, so I went in my purse, pulled my gun, and was seconds away from killing all of them."

"Did you do it?" She asked.

"I couldn't, but I wanted to."

"What stopped you?"

"I don't deserve to be in jail. My dad deserved to be there. Not me. I'm nothing like him."

"At that horrific time in your life, you talked yourself out of a situation by reminding yourself that you are a good person. See, just because unfortunate situations happen doesn't define who you are as a woman. You are not your dad. You are not your mom. You are not your ex-boyfriend Edward. You are not the people who have wronged you, and you don't have to keep carrying that heavy load. Let them suffer with the guilt of what they've done to you. Pick it up off of your chest and throw that crap on their chest. That load will forever be heavy if you don't muster up the strength and courage to get it off you."

I nodded my head and continued to cry. This shit felt like a ton of weight being lifted from my chest. I have been carrying this all of my life. Doctor Shonda has been a great listener. I didn't feel attacked or ignored. I needed this.

"So after Edward, did you ever enter into a new relationship or date anybody for a little while?"

"It happened last year. I called my best friend Keyshia, who has been like a blood sister to me. She rushed over, stopping her date with her boyfriend to console me. I went to her house and stayed with her for a few days to get my mind right. It's something I always did when I didn't feel stable. She has always been my backbone since a kid. That night her boyfriend invited over his friend, and we all had a good time, played cards, and enjoyed ourselves. I didn't know then that I would have met the love of my life. His name is Mike, and today he broke up with me."

"This is getting good. Now, what was Mike's reasoning for calling it quits?"

"He said that I continue to hurt the people that love

me. I need to get help and fix my trauma because I have pushed him away."

"Do you think you pushed him away?"

"He knows what I been through. I have always been an open book with him because I trust him. I don't understand why he feels like that."

"Was there an argument or a fight that led up to the breakup so we can unpack this?" She made a note in her journal.

"A week ago, we were supposed to have a date since we both were busy and had time that day. To my knowledge, we were supposed to go to dinner, but before we got to the restaurant, he took me to an open house to look for a place to move in together. We have been together for a year now. I feel like we were very much inseparable. The house was beautiful, but he wanted to submit an application to rent, and I simply said I wasn't ready yet. He blew up on me, and I hadn't heard from him until this afternoon when he broke up with me."

"How did you feel when it was time to submit the application?"

"I felt blindsided. I would have told him no if he had communicated that with me earlier in the day."

"Describe Mike to me. Be as descriptive and as open as you can be. I'm trying to understand him in my head."

I closed my eyes and pictured Mike. "Michael Simmons. He's a very tall, handsome man. I couldn't take my eyes off him from the first day I met him. He's quiet around people but very outspoken around me. He has a beautiful smile. He's loving. He's caring. He's hilarious. He's patient. He's an overthinker. I can't think of anything he wouldn't do for me. He has a daughter from a previous relationship, but I consider her my bonus child. He adores her, which is why I could see myself possibly having a child one day. He has changed my whole perspective on life. He knows how to love. He knows how to treat me with care and respect. That's all I could think of right now."

"Now, out of that list you gave me, do you see any problem with how the relationship could have gone left?"

"No, I don't." I honestly didn't understand.

"Maybe he is so patient with you because he wants to be with you. You saying you aren't ready probably made him feel unwanted and pushed away by you. If he respects your boundaries, do you respect his? Do you even know what his boundaries are regarding the relationship?"

"I can't see that, though. I love him, and we mutually know there's love on both ends. I show him that regularly. I just don't understand how he could feel pushed away. I cater to him. I respect him. I'm on his side."

"Yes, you may show him that, but you also said he is an overthinker. His love language may not only be physical from what you do, but it may be mental from how you make him feel. He may show you a smile and is hurting inside. You could love a person so much, but the same person can also drain so much out of you. Men are different from women. He may not show his emotions as women sometimes cannot keep a straight face. A lot of the time, it's a pride thing or feeling like he can't express himself. That's why it's important to keep a safe space between each other, so when something is on either of your minds, it could be talked out, and neither of you can walk away feeling attacked."

"Am I a burden to him?"

"Honestly, you won't know until he tells you that himself. He may just feel like his end of the relationship isn't being reciprocated. If you say he is putting in overtime to make your mind feel at ease and you are doing overtime to make his living day to day feel plush you two aren't doing the same type of work."

"I have to figure this out." I felt blown away.

"Are you guys completely over, or is this a break?"

"His actions say we are completely over, but his words say it's a break. He seems very much hurt too."

"Well, let's see if we can get him to join one of our sessions and see what we can unpack together. That way, he could tell you how he feels, and you can let him know it's not what he thinks."

"Hopefully, he would come."

"If he loves you and wants it to work too, he will, and that's the answer you need right there."

An hour went by fast. I scheduled my next session for next week and felt somewhat better. I left and picked up some Mexican food by my house so I could relax and continue to unpack these emotions for my next session. I'm going back and forth with my heart if I want to go to Kiki's birthday party in a couple of days. I don't know if I'm ready to face him so soon, but I don't want to jeopardize my relationship with Kiki at the same time.

Chapter 5

Keyshia Wright

My heart sunk as Bully and I pulled up to the trampoline park for Kiki's birthday party. I felt so weird coming, and Erin isn't here. I have grown to love Kiki since she's around all the time. She and Bully have a tight relationship, and he takes his role as her godfather seriously. I'm happy to be here to celebrate her on her special day. What I'm not pleased about is Mike breaking things off with Erin. Especially since I'm here right now and I have never met his baby mama before. I wouldn't mind dragging her over Erin, pregnant and all. That's what best friends are for.

Me: Are you sure you're not coming for Kiki? We just pulled up, and it's a lot of people here. Text me back, please!

I sent Erin a text. She had been ignoring all of my texts. I have known her damn near my whole life, and I've never seen her this hurt before. I don't think she even knew how much she loved Mike until he was done with the relationship. I am hoping that this is just a break and not anything permanent. I'm rooting for them. They're really meant for each other.

"Come on." Bully opened the car door for me.

"My bad." I half smiled. I was in my zone, not

paying attention to shit he said.

I followed behind him while he carried tons of gift bags and boxes for the birthday girl. As we walked in, I scanned the room. I saw no familiar faces except Mike, Kiki, Logic, and mama Lori. I sighed, seeing Erin hadn't texted me back. I walked over to Lori to greet my mother-in-law. She was with Mike's mom enjoying a cocktail.

"Hi, Keysh." She opened her arms for a hug and a peck on my cheek.

"Hey, mama. How are you, Ms. Simmons?" I hugged and greeted them both.

"My baby is growing so big and healthy." Mama Lori rubbed my belly. I melted inside.

Bully walked by at the same, and I followed behind him. I was out of place, so I was going to be where I felt the most comfortable. After pulling out my chair for me, we sat at one of the round tables along with Mike. I sat back and tuned them out while they talked. I wanted to get on Mike's head about their breakup, but this wasn't the time or place.

"Hi, uncle!" Kiki ran up from behind us, hugged Khalil, and hugged me. "Hi, auntie Keyshia."

"Happy birthday, beautiful!" I hugged her beautiful little self back.

Her eyes roamed the room before they fell back to the three of us. "Where's Erin?" She had a frown on her face.

"I'm sure she's just running late," I told her because these two fools weren't going to speak up.

"Tell her to come to find me. I want her to jump on the trampoline with me." Her bright smile resurfaced before she ran off.

"Okay!" I yelled, but I knew she couldn't hear me.

She and Erin had a close relationship too. Kiki is the sweetest, and it would be evil of you not to fall in love with her. She's super respectful, and even though I have beef with her mama because of the jealousy towards my best friend, she and Mike are doing a fantastic job raising her. For the twenty minutes I have been sitting here, I could see Kiki's mama grilling me. Bully pointed her out when we got here so I wouldn't start any shit, but I'm going to have to break my promise in a minute. She cannot keep her eyes off of me. I turned and bucked my eyes at her letting her know that I could clearly see her staring with her slow ass. She turned away like I didn't just catch her.

"I'll be right back," I said to Bully before getting up.

"Where are you going?" He frowned.

"To get some air and call Erin again."

He backed off. I needed to breathe because I hadn't been here long and was ready to go. When I got outside, I called Erin, and once again, it rang until the voicemail picked up. When I was about to go inside, her white BMW pulled up. I looked hard to make sure it was her through her tinted windows. I felt relieved when it was her exiting the car.

"Bitch I'ma cuss you the fuck out for ignoring me!" I walked over to her, helping with the gift bags she had brought.

"It's taking a lot of courage to show my face here today." She sighed.

The hurt was still very much in her hazel eyes. One thing I could say, though, is that my best friend didn't come to play with Mike or his baby mama. She's eating all these bitches up in here. Even though her outfit is appropriate for a children's party, her thick ass body took it over the edge. She wore a pair of distressed jeans, a nude crop top showing her belly button ring and tattoos, her Prada boots, and the bag to match. Her jewelry was blinding the fuck out of me, and I could tell that she had just got her hair laid because this was a new style from the last time I saw her. Her weave was damn near sweeping the ground. She looked beautiful. I know when Mike sees her, he's gonna wanna taste her day, but he won't be able to.

"Honestly, he looks just as sad as you. I was just sitting at the table with him and Khalil. Maybe you guys just need to talk." I tried to reason with her.

"We'll see, but for right now, it's about Kiki."

I agreed with her. I feel a lot better now since Erin came to join the party. I didn't want her to regret missing something special such as Kiki's birthday. If she and Mike ever rekindled their relationship, I wouldn't want Kiki resenting her because of things she wasn't old enough to understand. Together we entered the party, and I helped her put the gifts at the gift table directly in front of the table Mike and Bully were sitting at. She hugged Bully, and Mike even wanted to hug her too.

Sitting at the table was so awkward for like thirty minutes. We didn't say much as a group like we usually do, but once Erin got herself something to drink, she loosened up then Mike did too. The whole time he kept his eyes trained on her. It seemed like he wanted Bully and me to get up and give them some privacy. Outside looking in, you wouldn't have known they were currently broken up. The flames were still burning in both of their eyes.

"You okay?" I asked Erin once Mike and Bully got up from the table.

"I feel better now that I'm here." She smiled.

"I can't tell you guys haven't talked in a week."

"I thought the same thing too."

"You think he regrets it?" I asked.

"I don't know. Sometimes you never know with Mike. You can hardly ever read him, but he seems sincere."

"For sure. There goes Kiki." I pointed seeing her talk to her dad.

"Let me go over there." She got up from the table to join Kiki and Mike.

I sat back and watched everybody since I was at the table by myself. Kiki looked thoroughly happy to see Erin, and Mike had a big ol' grin on his face too. He was not just smiling like this until Erin got here. The three of them went on the trampoline together and seemed to have fun. I looked to my right, and his baby mama looked hurt. That girl still wanted Mike, and that was her problem. That man has moved on, and she's holding on to something that isn't there. I sat back and observed everybody.

Bully came back to the table, ending my nosiness. He sat a plate in front of me with pizza and wings. The pizza was alright, but I devoured the wings drenched in ranch. He knows exactly what I like.

"Uh-oh," I said, seeing Erin and Mike walk hand in hand to the maintenance room. I couldn't believe they were about to fuck right here.

Bully chuckled, but I don't know if it's funny or not. I'm overprotective about Erin; I know she loves Mike with all her heart. I honestly don't believe he has any ill intentions to break her heart, but if they can't figure out what they're doing, they shouldn't be randomly fucking. It's a dangerous game. Erin's mental health isn't as strong as other women. She can't handle what they can handle.

It takes little to nothing for her to snap and spiral, and this last year and a half, she has been doing so well and is finally off her medication.

"Just mind your business," Bully warned me before eating his food.

He was right. I talked to Bully in the meantime but was looking at the time on my phone. I was dying to know what was happening. I hope they were talking and not just fucking. I felt like a stalker, but I'm just rooting for them and want the best. They will have to see each other a lot since they're both KJ's godparents and our best friends. We are family regardless.

My eyes darted to the door when it opened. I watched them walk over to the restroom. I guess their slutty asses were cleaning themselves up. I laughed inside. Neither of them had any shame written on their faces. About fifteen minutes later, the two innocently walked back to the table as if nothing had happened, and I played along right with them.

I avoided asking Erin anything while we were still here at the party. I just wanted her to enjoy herself. We spent an hour and a half at the party, and I left with Erin. I was tired of hearing all of them damn kids yelling. I'm getting old now that unnecessary noise irritated me. We walked out of the party with Mike and Bully. My man needed to ensure I got to points A and B safely every time.

"Well, hello. Nice to see you here." Mike's baby mama walked up to Erin.

"I told you about that bullshit, Shana," Mike said to her.

"I'm just greeting her." She wanted to act all innocent now.

"Don't even speak to her. You ain't got shit to say

but start drama. Leave her the fuck alone and go enjoy this expensive ass party. Get out of her face." She looked defeated before storming back into the party like the child she was. Mike checked her, and I was happy to see that.

Bully opened the car door for me and left me with a juicy kiss. I was going out for dinner with Erin and planned to enjoy my Saturday night. I'm sure Bully wasn't coming home any time soon, and that's fine with me. I got in the car and waited for Mike and Erin to finish whatever they were doing. A couple of minutes later, she got in the car, and we drove off.

"Bitch, spill all the motherfuckin' tea! 'Cause I know y'all fucked." I got on her ass right away.

"You don't miss anything, do you?" She kept her eyes on the road.

"Spill it!"

"It's complicated for real. At first, it felt like everything was normal, but then we started talking, and all these emotions came out. He thanked me for coming. He said it meant a lot to him even though I wasn't obligated to come. Then we were just kissing and touching and fucked."

"That's it? Y'all not back together?"

"No, I don't think so. It seems like that's all it was."

"That was a waste of time. I've been waiting to hear what happened this whole time. He seemed like he was fully back into the relationship."

"That's what I'm talking about, Keyshia. He's confusing as fuck. He points the finger at me and says I throw mixed signals, but he does too."

"He for sure does." I agreed 'cause ain't no way Bully could try that with me. Don't dick me down then, leaving me more confused. There would be sugar in each of his tanks, a busted window, flattened tires, and I may even swing on his mama. Who knows?

Erin drove us to Eddie V's in Manhattan Beach. We continued our conversation about all the drama, and I informed her about the glares from his baby mama. When we got to the restaurant and were seated, I still wasn't done with what I had to say.

"I can't stand that bitch!" I finally said my peace.

"She's messy as hell."

"But she still has a thing for Mike, believe it or not."

"I know the bitch does, and he sees it too. That's why he stops her ass from the second she starts. Even though we aren't on good terms, I appreciate that because I would have never come if I felt like he was being funny to me. He never allowed the bullshit from the beginning. Since day one, he has made it clear that I am his woman, and she needs to respect it. We have no reason to say any words to each other. She was just being funny before we left because she had a crew of friends; this was the longest she had ever been in my presence. I know the bitch is stalking my social media."

"I agree that was some grown man shit he did. I would have looked at him differently if he tried to rub her in your face, but he has never been that type. He knows her best, so he nipped it in the bud." I took a forkful of my steak.

"It for sure wouldn't have been cool. She's only Kiki's mom. That's it, and that's all. I respect her for that but keep the bitch away from me. We don't have shit to talk about at all, and Mike makes that clear as day. We don't see each other any other time than her birthday. Mike answers the door to keep us separated when she comes to pick her up at the house."

"Are you still getting those Unknown phone calls?" I asked.

"No, it stopped. Thank God."

"I'm still watching that bitch."

"She's watching too, trust me. She doesn't have a life." She said, drinking her martini. Gosh, I wish I could have had a drink with her.

Her phone buzzed. Unlocking her phone, she got a text from Mike.

"See, this is why it's confusing. Why is he texting me and asking about my whereabouts?" She genuinely looked confused.

"You fucked him good, and you came to the party eating all them hoes up! Now he can't get you off of his mind." I giggled.

"I'm ignoring him because I'm not playing these games with him. If he wanna fix our relationship, I'm open to it, but you not gonna move all your shit out of my place, break up with me, and still think you have a say-so over what I chose to do."

"I feel you on that one! He's still sprung, though. Y'all have had deep chemistry since the day we were at my house, and y'all met. I knew from then y'all would eventually hook up. You guys couldn't keep your eyes off of each other." I smiled thinking about that night I ran up on Bully, ready to square up over nothing. It's funny to laugh at now since we are married and living our best life.

I received a text from Bully asking me to bring him a plate home. I was going to do that anyway.

"I guess they're not having fun 'cause why are they both texting us?" I laughed.

"When it's our turn to go out, they wanna blow up

our phones and shit. I'm not texting this man back at all. Cry about it 'cause you didn't give a fuck when I've been calling all last week."

"Well then." I looked at her sideways. She was still venting. At this point, their shit was so confusing that they didn't even know what was happening.

"I'm just playing his game." She shrugged.

We ate our dinner and enjoyed each other's company. Erin had one too many drinks. I didn't judge. From the week she had, Lord knows she needed it. When we left, I drove home so she could sober up. I made her come inside with me.

"What if he pops up right now with Bully when he comes home?" She said.

"I'm sure it's possible that could happen." Since Mike is always around.

"I'ma act like I have a date."

"You think that's going to work?"

"I don't know, but if he comes, play along and don't leave me looking stupid."

"Sure thing." I hope for her sake it doesn't backfire on her.

We went upstairs to my bedroom to chill until she was sober enough. For an hour and a half, we talked shit and laughed our assess off. By now, she had come down from being tipsy and was very coherent. I know the difference with her. The front door opened, and I could hear Bully talking to Mike. Just as she predicted, he ended up coming. I was laughing on the inside because this was about to be messy.

"Bitch I told you!" She was excited like she had made a touchdown.

"Come on!"

She arranged her clothes and applied more lip gloss to her lips before we walked down the stairs. She started a conversation that threw me off guard. I forgot that we were acting. This bitch is so damn crazy. I think my friend is a professional liar because she easily snapped into character.

"He said he was okay coming over this late, so I need to hurry up." This bitch was a natural.

"Alright, be safe. Let me know how it goes." I giggled, indulging in the conversation with her.

"Did I show you his picture?" She showed me nothing on her phone, but I pretended as if it was someone.

By the time we got to the bottom of the staircase, Mike had a scowl. Saying he was pissed was an understatement. That nigga wanted to snatch her phone.

"You wasn't gonna text me back?" He had an attitude towards her.

"For what?" She shrugged. "Love you, Keysh. See you later KJ." She rubbed my belly before walking to the door to leave. I followed behind her to walk her out.

"Erin!" His voice was stern. I stopped in my tracks as if he was talking to me.

"I gotta go, alright? I'll see you when I see you." She walked out of the house, got into her car, and drove off. He looked like he wanted to beat her ass. I haven't seen him this mad before. He was in his feelings.

"She for real?" He turned to ask me.

"Seems like it." I shrugged. "I mean, I can't talk her out of anything. She is a grown woman, and she's not tryna hear me." I said to pick at his brain. "You did end things with her leaving her to do what she wants." He was falling right into my trap. Men are so stupid sometimes.

"Didn't I tell you to stay out of their business?" Bully came into the foyer.

"Mike asked." I shrugged, walking up the stairs to eavesdrop.

I didn't hear much of Mike talking. Bully kept telling him not to worry about it. Mike has never been this quiet before. He for sure was hurt, and her game worked. I went into the bathroom and locked the door to call Erin.

"Hello," I whispered.

"Did he fall for it?" She asked.

"Bitch he is pissed!" She couldn't stop laughing.

"That's what his ass gets."

"What if he goes over there after he leaves here?" I asked.

"I'm just not going to answer. He can't come over. I don't give a fuck."

"Text me when you get home, so I know you made it in safe. I'ma keep you updated when he leaves. I'm trying to hear what they are talking about."

"Alright." We hung up the phone, and I went back to spying. I laughed inside, seeing Mike upset. He deserved it for fucking with my girl. He needs this dose of his own medicine. That video on Logic's Instagram story looked really bad. I know for a fact it messed Erin up too. The difference is he probably fucked that stripper. The bitch looked like she had just hit a lick, and Mike's intoxicated ass didn't see it in her sly ass. Erin only made up this fake story to get back at his ass for that.

Chapter 6

Khalil "Bully" Wright

We landed in Miami and had an hour to make it to the check-in for our cruise. Keyshia wanted to go on a cruise or to Jamaica. We ended up finding a seven-day cruise that'll stop in the Caribbean. I was excited as fuck too. I couldn't wait to see what it was like outside of LA. I never got the chance to travel when April was alive. I thought we had our whole life ahead of us to do that type of shit. This was new to me, and I was excited to experience it.

Before we booked the cruise, we went to her doctor to ensure it was safe for her. Her doctor did recommend a couple of things for motion sickness. I wanted to make sure we were extra prepared. We flew through the airport to grab our luggage. I didn't want us to be late. Keyshia would have a fit if we couldn't board on time.

She ordered an Uber to take us to the ship. We made it in forty-five minutes, right when people started to get in line. She couldn't hide the smile on her face, and neither could I. This was some different shit for me. Being a hood nigga there weren't so many opportunities to do shit like this.

I know she needed the break, but I did too. I've been

under so much stress these last couple of weeks and have hardly been able to sleep since my mind hasn't turned off. KJ is due in a couple of months. We still haven't put together his room yet. I'm nervous as fuck about being a dad, but I can't tell Keyshia that. I wouldn't want her thinking it's because of April and our daughter Olivia. I just wrote off love and being a parent for three years after they passed away, so this is a lot happening all at once.

Keyshia didn't force me into this, but I'm still adjusting. My heart is traumatized as fuck. Not only did I lose my fiancé but our child as well in that fiery car crash. It took a lot to get up and push through. I'm happy that I met my wife and we got married. From the second she changed my mind and made me want to lock her ass down, I knew she was the one for me. It's not a second thought at all, but I know her mind works, and if I tell her the truth about being nervous, she'll come up with some assumption in her head.

I'm still trying to accept Keyshia and KJ as a part of my future, if that makes sense. You don't know what it's like to go about your typical day thinking you'll come back home to your family only to get a phone call, and you lose your whole world for no reason. I'm sure it'll leave some scars and bruises on you too. It's not a day that goes by where I don't think about April and our baby and what our life would have been like. Regardless of me moving on and creating a new family, April and Olivia's death shouldn't have gone down like that. To this very day, I wish I could have replaced their lives with mine.

The club has added on more stress than a little. I took on way more than I thought I could handle. The club's opening is in two weeks, and I pray it's successful because I put a lot of money and time into this investment. Then I had Pamela on my hands. She was good at her job, but this bitch made me want to strangle her, and I'm sure Keyshia would like me to do it too.

I haven't seen or heard from Tori in a minute, and I'm hoping her dumb ass got the picture now. I've been trying to spare her, but if she can't get it together, the bitch will be gone. I can't have Keyshia being insecure about a bitch I don't even want.

I've been doing my best tryna keep Logic out of more trouble. Ever since the shooting, he calmed down from the crazy shit he was doing, but I feel like it is only a matter of time before he's back on his bullshit. He has a faithful track record of chilling out for a couple of weeks before he does something ignorant again.

"You good, babe?" Keyshia asked, breaking my thoughts.

"I'm good."

I opened my arms for her to hug me. I squeezed her without hurting the baby. We were next in line to board the ship. Keyshia scanned her phone with our ticket barcode, and we handed over our passports and ID's. Once everything was good, the man gave us our room keycard and took our luggage. We walked around the big ass ship to find our suite. This shit was huge as a motherfucka. I know I'ma get loss on here. We finally found our suite, and our shit was extravagant as fuck. I didn't even think cruise ships could look like this. We had a huge room that could fit a whole family. We didn't need all of this space, but I didn't like to feel claustrophobic. We had a balcony and two hot tubs. I'ma be using that shit for sure.

Once Keyshia made sure that the WiFi we paid for worked, we went to explore the ship. There was so much to do in the next seven days. I don't know how we would get it all done before then. I'ma have to come back again. I know the rest of our family would enjoy this too.

"I'm hungry. Let's go find me something to eat." I followed Keyshia out of the suite. Whatever she needed. We ended up at one of the restaurants. I didn't expect much of this, but I was impressed when my steak and lobster came to the table. I didn't think this would be fine dining, but I was wrong. Keyshia and I fucked up everything we ordered.

"I probably shouldn't bring this up, but it was on my mind. April's mama texted me yesterday to check on me. I didn't reply because I didn't know what to say really."

"Does she always check on you?" She asked.

"We kept in touch after April passed away. She and my mom are still close, but I've stopped replying since we've been together. My mama says she doesn't know what to say to her either."

"You can text the lady back, Khalil. She probably still feels like April is alive when she speaks to you. That was a tragic way to die; a mother's heart will forever mourn her child."

"You cool with that?" She sounded hella mature, and this is not the wife I married.

"It's nothing to be upset about. Now it would be different if April was alive and you two were just broken up. You know some mama's be tryna be funny."

I switched the conversation because I didn't want to talk about it the whole trip. I didn't wanna think about shit that was back in LA. I could deal with it when I got home. Right now, I just wanted to slide into my wife's good ass pussy and enjoy all this shit.

"Another drink on the house, sir." The waiter

brought another glass of Casamigos to me.

After lunch, we went back to our suite to wait for our luggage. I didn't want my shit sitting at the door so anybody could snatch it. I would get kicked off today before the ship even sails off. We didn't have to wait long. It came fast once we had gotten back. We both took a shower and chilled in the room. Before we enjoyed our night, Keyshia was tired and needed to get off her feet.

Chapter 7

Michael "Mike" Simmons

While Bully is on his honeymoon, I gotta handle everything here with minimal help from Logic. We didn't let his careless ass do too much. I had just pulled up to the gas station to check on our business, but my phone rang before I got out of my truck. I shook my head, seeing Erin's name and picture on my screen. I haven't heard from her since Kiki's birthday two weeks ago. She had been dodging me at the club, so I kept my distance. I know she intended to make me jealous and mad. I could give it to her, though, 'cause she for sure got me mad that night at Bully's crib. I blew her phone up for two days after that, and I didn't get a call back or text message reply, so I already knew what she was on.

"Wassup, what you need, E?" I answered the phone and got back in the truck for privacy.

"Hey, Mike. I'm calling because I have been going to therapy, and my therapist suggested that it would be healthy for me to have you join one of my sessions if that is okay with you."

I was shocked but happy for her. Despite what she may believe, I still love her and will support her in anything she does. Erin is a good woman. She was just dealt some fucked up cards. Until she can learn to heal and move forward, I just gotta be on the side.

"Yeah, I'll come to support you."

"Really? I thought you would have said no."

"What would make you think that?"

"We aren't on the best of terms right now."

"Nah, we good. I told you that. I just want you to heal."

"It's today at 4 pm. I hope it's not too last minute. I was hesitant to call and ask."

"Text me the address, and I'll be there."

Looking at the time on the dashboard, it was already after one, and I had to quickly wrap this up so I could go home and change. We hung up, and I received the text right away. I got out of the car and made sure all of the niggas standing out front were doing what they were supposed to do and not causing any attention. I walked inside and used my key to get into the hidden office. Everything was just how I left it yesterday. I didn't have to do count until tomorrow, so I gladly left after ensuring everything was on point. I made it home at about 2:30 pm. I smoked a blunt on my way here so I could just shower and get dressed.

I went into my closet first to see what I wanted to wear. Once I picked it out, I took my time in the shower. I was mentally trying to prepare myself to see Erin, especially since it was a therapy session. I knew this would take a lot of emotions out of me, but I'd do it for her.

Once I showered, I washed my face and brushed my teeth before getting dressed. I felt like I was dragging my feet, but I knew for sure I had to do this for her. If she needed this from me so she could heal, I wouldn't rob her of that. Somebody in her life had to put her first for once. We will always be around each other regardless of our relationship due to Keyshia and Bully. I'm not tryna hate her, especially since I always have to see her.

I made it out of the house thirty minutes before her session. I tried to get there on time but made it five minutes late. I got out of the car and made it inside. The receptionist escorted me inside the office. Erin was sitting on the couch and looking beautiful as fuck. She did look nervous. The therapist stood up and greeted me, and I hugged Erin before sitting beside her.

"I'm so glad you could make it, Mike." I nodded at the therapist. "So, this is Erin's third session with me, and I feel like we're making some progress, right?" She looked at Erin.

"Agree. I wanted you to come because I value you and your opinion. I want to be able to speak to you openly, but I know that sometimes I don't process things the correct way. Bear with me, please, and be open if you can." Erin half smiled.

"In our first session, Erin gave me a very descriptive list of you and your characteristics. We used that list to try and dig into the reasoning behind the separation to let her see her trauma. Now that you are here, could you provide her with the answers to her questions?"

"Where do we start?" I asked.

"Mike, do you often feel pushed away, or do your opinions and emotions not matter in the relationship with Erin?" She asked.

"Yes." I truthfully answered.

"Do you often cover your feelings to not push the buttons with her trauma?"

"Yes."

"Could you look at Erin and explain how you feel pushed away or unheard? Erin, please use this time to listen and not interrupt Mike. You'll have your turn to speak."

"When we met, you showed me your scars. I could have walked away from the beginning because I knew it was a lot. But we connected, and I knew that you weren't a bad person. You were just lost. I thought you were building a better relationship with yourself in the beginning. Towards the middle of our relationship, you stopped because you got comfortable with the happiness we had together. It overshadowed your past, so you didn't see the trauma anymore. Just because you didn't see it with your eyes doesn't mean you didn't make me feel it, though."

"I always want you to know, Mike, that hurt people hurt people. Meaning sometimes it's unintentional, and I think in Erin's case, from getting to know her, she doesn't see that she wears her trauma on her sleeve."

"That's why I tried to be patient with her. I've tried to be gentle as I can. I don't raise my voice or move in ways that she could think I would harm her. It's like walking on eggshells. Don't get me wrong, E, you are a great ass person. I love you. I'm still in love with you, but I'm tired of being treated like I'm the one who hurt you. You subconsciously do it all the time.

The shit that blew me is you refuse to allow us to have our names together on a lease or deed, but you're cool with me sleeping with you every night and paying every bill. I have never controlled you. When I left, you saw you still had every gift I ever paid for. I'm not the nigga that's gonna take shit back from you. I don't embarrass you or abuse you. I don't understand how coming together under one roof is too much for you when we do it daily. You want me to be your man but won't step out of my way so I can be the man. I feel like you don't want to heal, so you'll use the excuse that you're not ready forever, and I don't have that type of time."

"Erin, you can speak." The therapist said.

"I am so sorry, Mike. From the bottom of my heart, I am sorry. I am in love with you! I never tried to hurt you purposely. I thought I was protecting our relationship by not moving in with you. I feel like everything goes wrong when I get close to anyone. I didn't want to risk our relationship by committing in that way."

"I've been serious about you since day one. You are the only woman Kiki has met. She knows you as her stepmom. My baby loves you the way she loves her mama. It hurts to see that you still don't recognize me as a good man. You make me feel like I should have cheated on you. I should have been a dog because what's the difference with how you treat a dog or a good man?"

"I'm sorry." She cried hysterically.

"Look, I'm not bashing you. Even after all that, I still love you, girl." I wiped her tears away.

"You are the only man I could say I ever loved, Mike. You challenge me to grow, and that's why I push away so much because I'm scared of growth."

"You are so scared of growth that you push away your future, Erin. I wanna marry you. I wanna have kids with you. I wanna put your mind at ease. I don't want you to be submissive. That is a triggering word that's a part of your trauma. I want you to be happy so that I can be happy. I want us to both put in work together, but you have to heal first."

"I'm trying." She wiped away her tears.

"Thank you, Mike, for joining us. I feel like this is an eye opener for you, Erin." The therapist said.

"Before we're done, let me say one more thing. I understand a lot more than I did three weeks ago. Thank you for breaking up with me. It made me want better for myself, but that has to do with your positive influence on me. I apologize for treating you like my abusers. You are in no way, shape, or form anything like them. You are an amazing man, and truly I don't deserve you. I'm still a little girl inside, healing from all the hurt. Please forgive me one day."

"I forgive you now, Erin."

"Can we at least be friends? I hate not hearing your voice every day. It's killing me."

"It's killing me too."

She smiled, and I did too. The therapist dismissed me, and I left out of the building and waited in my truck for her. We both needed this. We have had many talks in our relationship, but this was the first time we listened to each other. Hopefully, this is the right step in the right direction. Truthfully, I missed my girl. I missed her cooking, lying in bed with her, and the sex between us.

Erin came out of the building about thirty minutes later. Her face was down, texting on her phone. I'm not sure if she saw me in the truck or not, so I got out to greet her. When she looked up, she paused and continued walking my way. I opened my arms for a hug.

"I'm proud of you!" Truly I am.

"Thank you for always having my back."

"It's forever with us." It felt good to have her back in my arms. "Can I take you out to dinner?"

"I would love that, but I cooked dinner before coming here. You can come over. You are always welcomed."

"I rather your cooking anyways."

I helped her into her car and then followed her to her apartment. We made it there in twenty minutes. I parked in my usual parking spot and followed behind her as she unlocked her door. There was an eerie feeling I suddenly got.

"Wait, hold on." I took her key to open the door. I told her to wait at the door, so I could go inside to check first. I walked through each room, and nothing looked out of place, but something felt strange. I'm from the streets, so I know I'm not wrong with my intuition.

"You haven't had anybody here?" I asked her when I went to get her from the door.

"Nah." She replied.

"Something ain't right in here, E. You still are getting those unknown phone calls?" I questioned.

"It stopped for about a month, but a few days ago, I got one call." She shrugged it off.

"Somebody was in here, Erin. I'm right about a lot of shit, and I know for a fact I'm right about this one too. Go check yo' shit in the closet."

Her face looked worried. I went into the room with her while she made sure nothing was missing. I saw her trace her steps, confirming that someone was in here.

"What's missing?" I asked.

"My diamond earrings. I placed it in my earring case earlier while I was cleaning. It's not here, and I am positive I did because I was on FaceTime with Keyshia when I did it. I was showing her the new case I bought and how I organized it."

"You coming home with me tonight." I was serious. I'd never leave her alone, knowing there's potential danger. I'd go crazy if I ignored it and let her be home alone and something happened to her.

I pulled up my phone and called Rell. He is one of our runners. I made him go to Best Buy and get a Ring camera and a drill for me to put on her door. Erin lived on the fourteenth floor, so somebody entered through the front door.

"I'ma set up a camera and see what's going on. I told you that you should have gotten one."

"I'm pretty sure it's nobody but your baby mama stalking me."

"Shana is an annoying bitch, but she ain't got enough balls to break into your shit knowing I'd fuck her up. This ain't Shana, Erin. It's somebody else. How would she even get access to your building?"

While I waited for Rell to show up, I helped Erin pack. I don't know what it meant for our relationship, but I'd rather her be safe at home with me. She looked like she had something to say but didn't want to. I know my girl and could clearly see something was on her mind.

"What E? Say what's on your mind. It's bothering you."

"Did you sleep with that stripper?" She quizzed.

"Wait. What?" What the fuck was she talking about?

"You had that bitch ass all in your face at the strip club the same day you decided to stop answering all of my calls."

"Nah, I didn't fuck her." I simply said.

"You didn't?" She looked like she didn't believe me.

"When have I lied? How the fuck you know I was at the club anyways?"

"I have my sources."

"Why are you questioning me when you were out on dates just two weeks ago? It could have been that nigga who broke into your house."

"I wanted to make you jealous. There was no date I came straight home; Keyshia was in on it if you don't believe me."

I don't know why it felt good to know she lied. I was jealous like a motherfucka that night.

"Well, you did," I admitted to her.

"You had me all confused. You broke up with me, and then you fuck me at your daughter's birthday party."

"I can't resist you, Erin. You are making it seem like I don't love you. The only reason why you are talking to a therapist right now is because we broke up. So clearly, the breakup helped in some way."

Before she could reply, my phone rang. Rell called to let me know he was at the gate. I rushed downstairs to meet him. I couldn't wait to set the camera up and see who it was. A person with a motive will always come back. Erin got a lot of designer shit. For one earring to be missing was a red flag. A thief would have taken everything. Whoever it was known their way around her building.

"You good, bro?" Rell asked.

"Yeah, good looking." I took the bag from him and went back upstairs.

Immediately I unboxed the camera and connected it to my app. I wanted these alerts to be sent directly to my phone. I had the camera set up in less than fifteen minutes. Once my mind felt a little at ease, I grabbed her two suitcases for us to leave.

"Wait, what about the food?" She asked.

"I don't trust it. Whoever it was could have

poisoned it."

"Are you sure we aren't being too dramatic?"

"Let me do what I do, Erin."

We left, and I placed her suitcases in my trunk. She followed me to my house. A nigga was low-key happy she was coming back home with me. I meant that I missed her being in my space. I had gotten used to having her around for so long that not talking or being around her every day felt weird as fuck.

We made it to my house in thirty minutes. I told her to park her car in the garage while I took the suitcases into the house. I was in and out. I wanted to take her out to dinner since that was the plan originally. I helped her into the front seat of my truck before I got in.

"Where are we going?" She asked.

"Crustacean's." It was one of her favorite Asian restaurants in Beverly Hills.

"I could have cooked."

"It's nothing in that refrigerator," I admitted.

"Seriously, we have to stop at the grocery store before going home." She scolded me.

"Alright."

She smiled, and her sexy ass hazel eyes sparkled. I haven't seen her smile like this since I met her earlier. Shit, I was smiling too. When we finally made it to the restaurant, it wasn't crowded for it to be a Wednesday night. There was open seating, so I picked the booth at the center of the dimly lit restaurant.

"Thank you," Erin said when she slid into the booth.

"For what?" I questioned.

"For always having my back."

I pulled her close and kissed her glossy lips. No

matter what we go through, I will be with her forever. It's just some shit we have to fix right now so we can spend the rest of our lives in peace. Before Erin stepped into my life, I had no female drama. My shit has always been peaceful, and I want the same for her.

We ordered our drinks and food. I listened to her open up about her therapy sessions. I can admit that I do hear the growth in her conversations. I'm really happy for her. Also, I'm glad I decided to come and support. I don't know what Erin would have walked back into when she got home if I wasn't with her. Shit, I don't know how long since I moved out all of this shit has been happening. I'll get to the bottom of it soon.

Chapter 8

Erin Jackson

I sighed, parking my car in front of Mike's beautiful home. I wanted to walk inside and put my pussy in his face. I have been so horny that I'm starting to feel miserable. The withdrawals were killing me slowly. I appreciate that he always support me but now, holding out on intimacy is no longer support its cruelty. He wanted to be careful with my feelings while I was on my journey to healing. I can't help that my panties soak up every time I stare or think about him. I grabbed my book bag and got out of the car before using my key to enter the house. He was sitting at the kitchen table eating Chinese take-out.

"Wassup E?" He was fucking his plate up. It smelled good too.

"I'm just E?"

"Wassup, babe, does that sound better?"

"Yes, it does. Hi babe."

I walked over to him to place a kiss on his lips.

"Are you hungry?" He asked.

"Yes, your food smells amazing."

"Your plate is in the microwave."

I smiled. He never ate without me. We bonded over

food. It doesn't matter the time of the day or the distance we'll travel for some good ass food and fuck it up. I appreciated the gesture of him always remembering the little things. Not to bring Edward up, but he'd come home with food for himself with the money I would give him. That shit used to break me down. I washed my hands and warmed up my food before sitting with him.

"How was school?" He asked.

"It was good. I'll have my certificate soon." I tooted my own horn.

I have always wanted to be a dentist since I was a kid. I love teeth, and I have a set of pearly whites. To be honest, I don't know what my obsession is, but it's something I have always wanted to do. Even though I don't have the patience to be in school for many years to become a dentist, a dental assistant is the best route for me. My ten-month program is some crucial shit. It's a lot of pressure and studying, but I feel like I am built for this shit. I have three months left until my final test. Once I pass it, I'll be certified and have the credential to work wherever I want to.

I've been looking for private pediatric dentists. The pay is higher, and I rather work with children. I met a dentist in the mid-city area that took a liking to me. She said if I followed through with my program, I needed to provide my certificate and documents, and she might have a spot for me. She said it with a wink, so I think I have a job lined up. I'm just so proud of myself.

"We gonna celebrate hard. I'm proud of you for real. This is big for you!"

"Man, this is big. I never thought I'd be anything but a bottle girl."

"That shows you that you can achieve anything

you put your mind to.”

“Facts.” I took a big bite of my food.

“I’m taking Kiki to the movies tonight. Do you wanna come with us?”

“I’d love to. Plus, she already invited me.” I giggled.

Kiki and I had an amazing relationship. I’m glad she knows I love her and her daddy. I love the amazing relationship she has with him. It’s something I always wished I had as a child, which is a far cry from my tragic childhood. Mike will create a bloodbath for anyone that harms his baby girl, and I love it.

“She texts you more than she calls me.”

“We text every day. I love it, though. She knows she’s special to me.”

“How is the therapy helping with us having kids? I know that was something you weren’t ready for.” He asked.

“I mean, it’s something I am facing by talking about it. I didn’t even want to hear my name in the same sentence with having my own child. It’s just a bunch of trauma I’m working through. I’m feeling okay, though. It’s not as bad as it used to be. I know I am capable of being a good mom to somebody one day. Having Kiki around helps me process it, then knowing I’ll be the godparent to KJ helps.”

It felt good as fuck to say out loud. Not having mentally stable parents that cared about my well-being broke me. I grew up feeling unloved. I would do anything to feel some sort of love because I had never had it before. I didn’t want a child because I don’t know how to be a parent since I’ve never had one. Then Mike came into my life, and I started to think maybe one day I could really do this parenting shit.

"You got it."

I smiled. I couldn't imagine having this conversation with anybody else but him. He is rooting for me to heal and be the best version of myself. I pray everybody who felt as lost as I did find someone who can love them as Mike loves me. This man feels like a second chance at life. I'm learning to not live through him but live on my own so that we can build a happy and healthy relationship together. I'ma spazz on anybody behind him.

"Enough of me. How are you?" I asked.

"I'm just happy you are back around with a clear mind. It feels good to have a real conversation with you, and I don't have to feel like you took your problems out on me."

"I'm glad I could catch myself before losing you."

"Did your views change about us living together?"

"Yes. It changed the second you broke up with me. I don't wanna lose you; I'ma say it over and over. You are my dog. We have a bond. I felt empty when we weren't speaking, and it killed me not to see you."

"I felt the same way."

"So why haven't we been intimate in the last week?" I just wanted to hear it out of his mouth.

"I'm not tryna let this dick mess with your healing." I laughed so hard, but he was serious. "You think I'm joking, but I'm not. I know my woman. You fiend over this dick, and I don't want you to get off track and forget about the big steps you have to take to reach your happiness."

"You think I'ma stop working on healing our relationship?"

"Yeah."

"I promise I won't. You already taught me that you

aren't playing with me."

"Don't say it like that. We just got shit to work on together."

"So, are we together now?"

"You always gonna be mine, Erin. We together, babe, since you need to hear it."

I smiled because I needed the reassurance. I closed my food container and stood up to go upstairs and shower. He was about to give me some dick and stop playing with me. I wanted to wash off because I hate getting in my bed with my outside clothes on.

"Be upstairs in fifteen minutes nigga. I'm not gonna keep begging you to hand me some of my dick." I yelled from upstairs, laughing. I loved our relationship, but I was dead ass serious too.

I went into the bathroom and undressed from my scrubs before wrapping my hair into my bonnet. My braids were freshly done, and I didn't want them soaking wet. I slipped into the shower and scrubbed my body thoroughly. Mike came into the shower with me as I was about to get out. It felt so good to be back in his arms and on good terms. We passionately kissed under the water. I helped scrub his back while he scrubbed the rest of his body. I got out first to dry off and remove my bonnet. I grabbed the lotion off the dresser before walking to the bed. Mike entered the room right after me. He laid on his back, and I poured lotion all over his chocolate body, allowing my hands to roam free and massage him. He looked so relaxed before my mouth swallowed his dick whole. I missed everything about his dick. I took every inch of him into my wet mouth, bobbing my head up and down his shaft. My man is no punk, but I was sucking the cum right out of his dick. His shit was dripping with precum.

"Alright, stop playing with me." He quickly got me off him and returned the favor by demolishing my pussy.

I moaned while grinding my hips onto his face. It was so passionate. Definitely, some make up sex. When I came into his mouth, he stood up and slipped inside of me, pinning both of my legs behind my head. He drilled my pussy so hard and fast, just like I wanted it. Not even five minutes in, my eyes rolled to the back of my head before I creamed all over him. Hearing him grunt, he did the same too. He collapsed right on the bed with me. That shit was good as fuck.

"And that's why I'm getting my shit together because you're not about to be fucking bitches giving them my dick!" I damn near yelled at him.

"I told you your crazy was gonna come out."

"No, that's my truth."

He got off the bed to grab a washcloth to clean me up. Once he was done, he laid back down, and I got up to get in the shower again. I didn't want to be sticky. I was out in like ten minutes. When I returned to the room, he was on the bed snoring. A grin appeared on my face. I missed knocking him out after sex. I got into bed right with him, cuddling.

I wanted to fall asleep, but I couldn't. I felt energized and thrilled since I got the dick I'd been waiting to taste. I grabbed my phone and pulled up the Ring camera app. I haven't looked at all the activity in front of my condo since yesterday afternoon. I scrolled until it played the last video I remembered seeing. I went through each video until one specifically caught my eye. I played it over and over, and my suspicions seemed correct. Edward walked to my door with a hood on, but he saw my camera and walked off. His face is in plain sight.

That motherfucka is the one stalking me! How? How the fuck do you do me dirty but want to stalk me? I got off the bed and paced back and forth, waiting for Mike to wake up. Knowing who it is behind the unknown calls and the break in at my condo makes me feel better. I've been on edge for a week since Mike wasn't letting this shit go. It was fucking bum ass, Edward. Mike woke up from his nap, hearing me pace.

"What happened?" He jumped up.

"Look!" I jumped on the bed showing him my phone.

"I told you they'll come back. You know who it is?" He asked.

"Edward, my ex."

"The one you were about to kill?"

"Yes."

"Mmm." He had a sinister look on his face.

"I'ma handle it, baby."

"That's who has been calling me!"

"We gonna go to Verizon and get your number changed. This really ain't nothing to worry about. This is some lightweight shit. You not going back to the condo without me. Stay here until it's cool, alright?"

I couldn't read his face. He was expressionless. I know my man didn't play about me, so I know he was going to fuck Edward up and about damn time. He said it was cool, so I'ma just leave the situation alone and let him handle it. I'm going to keep my eye out, though.

"Let's get up. I gotta pick Kiki up at six." He said, checking the time on his phone.

He walked off to take another shower, and I looked through the clothes I had here. I brought a lot in my two suitcases, but I need more clothes from my condo. I wore a pair of distressed jeans, a ripped Gallery Dept. t-shirt, and a pair of Nike Dunks to match. I topped it off with my makeup and jewelry. I decided on my Louis Vuitton handbag to match. I laid my baby hair down and was ready to go. Mike was finishing his last touches to his outfit. We walked to the garage together, and he decided on his Lamborghini Urus.

"You look sexy as fuck, babe." He said as he opened the door for me.

"Thank you, handsome. You look amazing as usual." I puckered my lips for him to kiss.

His diamond grill shined when he smiled. My man makes my pussy throb. He got in the car and drove off to pick Kiki up. We quickly made it to his baby mama's house. He parked in the driveway and quickly exited. I had no desire to be around his baby mama, so I scrolled through Instagram while he went to get his baby. They both made it back to the car in less than five minutes. Kiki flung open the passenger door to greet me with a hug. My heart smiled.

"Hey, Kiki." I hugged her tightly.

"I missed you!"

"I missed you more, but we gonna kick it tonight."

"Daddy said we can do whatever we want this weekend."

"Well, daddy is correct."

She got in the back seat, and Mike drove off to a movie theater in Glendale. The whole car ride Kiki kept us entertained. We talked about school, fashion, and all the things she liked. I really loved this little girl. With traffic, we made it to Glendale in about forty-five minutes. I gave Mike my phone for him to take pictures of Kiki and me in front of the truck. Then Kiki took pictures of Mike and me before I took pictures of her and her daddy together. It was a beautiful outing, and I was already enjoying my time.

When we got to the window to purchase the movie tickets, Kiki swore she could handle a scary movie. Mike never denied her of anything, so he gave in to her request. Before we went into the theater, we stopped to get snacks from the concession stand. Once the movie started, I dozed off. I woke up here and there hearing people yell from the scary scenes.

After the movie, we went to dinner. Kiki picked Sugar Factory because she wanted one of the cool drinks. When we got there, we had to wait a little while. As we stayed in the waiting area, we talked.

"I love you, Erin." Kiki randomly said.

"I love you too, Kiki." I pulled her in for a tight hug.

"You make my daddy happy." She hugged his arm.

"You and your daddy both make me happy." She innocently smiled when I told her that.

Mike and I looked at each other before kissing. I love them so much. For the first time, I felt like I have my own family, and I never want to be in jeopardy of losing them again. When we get home later, Mike and I have to talk. I'm ready now more than ever to go all the way with our relationship. Let's make us living under one roof official. I'm tired of being alone. I choose them.

When we finally got to our table, we already knew what to order. Kiki took a bunch of pictures and made videos for her TikTok. I enjoyed my outing and seeing the smiles on both her and Mike's faces. It made me want to push to heal so we can add a child to our family. In my mind, I reassured myself about ten times, saying that I am loved and needed.

After dinner, we went straight home. It was past time for Kiki to get in bed. Mike let her stay out long tonight, and she could barely keep her eyes open on the drive home. I helped her into her shower so she could sleep peacefully tonight while Mike and I continued to rekindle our love. Once she showered and changed into her pajamas, we both kissed her goodnight and closed her door. I went downstairs to grab two wine glasses while Mike turned on the music lowly.

"Here, babe." I sat on the couch next to him handing him his wine.

"Thank you." He took a sip.

"I want to sell my condo. I can't lose you again or Kiki."

"You ready for it?" He asked.

"I'm positive. Going out tonight was the confirmation that I needed. I'm in love with you, which has held us back for a long time. Whatever I have to do to fix us, I will do it without a doubt. We are in this forever." I wholeheartedly smiled, and he did too.

"You are healing." He was happy.

"All my life, I have been in panic mode, and in the last year and a half with you, I have been at peace. It was just second nature, which is why I often pushed you away. I'm stopping that shit because nothing can come between us again."

We talked for the remainder of the night. I even cried a little. We opened up about a lot of things and made plans for the future. It was time for me to put us first. The whole time it was one sided on my end. Now it's time to live in peace.

Chapter 9

Keyshia Wright

I felt like I was lying on a marshmallow bed when we returned home from our honeymoon. The cruise was such a vibe and a beautiful memory for us to share forever, but I missed being home. I didn't feel like getting up to get dressed for my doctor's appointment, but I was excited to see the ultrasound. I loved seeing my son grow and his development.

"What time is the appointment?" Bully walked into the bedroom, eating a sandwich.

"An hour and a half." I sighed, dreading the time.

"Get yo' ass up. About to make me late to see my son." He tried it before walking out of the room.

I used all of my strength to get out of bed. I walked past our suitcases and sighed. I have gotten so lazy lately. I was not thrilled to unpack and wash all our clothes from our trip. We had just gotten back late last night, and it took everything in me not to reschedule the doctor's appointment today. I went into the bathroom to shower quickly.

I didn't take a long time in the shower like I usually would have. I still didn't know what to wear, and being so tired, I moved very slowly. These days I had little to no effort in doing things. KJ was so heavy for me, only to be six months pregnant, that I chose to lay in bed all day or chill on the couch. Walking has not been a favorite activity of mine. I just ordered a belly band to help support his heavy self. Bully swears it's not KJ that's heavy. It's me eating too many lemon pepper wings. I beg to differ.

I dried off my wet body before brushing my teeth and hydrating my face with a quick facial. The weather change and the hormones had my skin feeling extra dry lately. Once satisfied, I quickly found an outfit to wear. It had to be something comfortable since I was meeting with Erin after my appointment. She said something was going on, but she couldn't say it over the phone while I was on the cruise. All I know is Bully and I will be going to Mike's house, which is in the complete opposite direction from her Downtown skyrise condo. I guess she and Mike are back together, and I love to see it!

"Babe!" I yelled for Bully to come here.

It took forever for his slow ass to meet me in my closet.

"You good?" He looked confused.

"You like this outfit?" I showed him what I picked out. It was cold today, and I hate cold weather.

"You look good in anything. Hurry up, though." He rushed me.

"You're never any help." I rolled my eyes.

I just wore the outfit. Another thing the hormones from this pregnancy have done to me is make me emotional and mean as hell. Some days Bully irks my soul. I damn near need a break away from him because I want to strangle him. I couldn't stand the rollercoaster of emotions.

I don't know if I was satisfied or not with my outfit, but I didn't have any time left to spare. I grabbed my purse and went downstairs so we could leave. I'm already hungry as hell, and Bully made me a sandwich, but I refused to eat the jailhouse concoction he made. I'll just wait until after the appointment to eat.

"You not gonna eat the sandwich?" He asked like I would have changed my mind.

"Dead serious. You are trying to poison me and my son."

He shook his head before placing it in the refrigerator. I made a mental note to throw it out when we returned home later. We left out of the house and drove to the doctor. KJ was in my belly doing backflips. We are just as excited to see him too.

We made it to the appointment in twenty minutes. We had to rush inside to make it right on time. The nurses checked me in and gave me a cup for my urine. I quickly gave them my urine sample and waited to be called. It didn't take longer than five minutes.

"Are you busy this weekend, bae?" Bully asked as he helped me lay back for my ultrasound.

"No, why?"

"Let's set up the nursery this weekend. I just want you around while I set the crib up."

"I thought you and Mike were going to do it together."

"He's still gonna help. I did a lot with helping when Kiki was born, so he gotta return the favor."

"Yes, I am excited! Finally, it's going to come together. We just have to get paint, but I'm unsure what color I want."

"We'll figure it out later."

I smiled because KJ's nursery is filled with nothing but shopping bags and unopened boxes and furniture. We have not done a single thing yet. Knowing that it'll finally come together this weekend gives me something to look forward to. There's still a lot more shopping to be done.

"How are you, Mr. and Mrs. Wright?" My doctor entered the room.

"We are great. How are you?" I greeted her.

"I'm great."

She did some things on her computer before grabbing the lube and rubbing it over my stomach, then proceeding with the ultrasound. KJ was on the screen covering his little face. He always hid his face covered whenever we did an ultrasound. Only a few times were we able to get clear shots of his face. The appointment lasted no longer than thirty minutes. We were in and out. Looking at the time on my phone, we had an hour before we had to be at the club. We had an appointment with a stylist Bully hired to style us for the club's grand opening. This was our second fitting for our alterations. On the way to the club, we stopped at In-N-Out because I couldn't wait any longer. I made a mess tearing this juicy ass burger up. There was nothing like a pregnancy craving.

Arriving at the club, Bully was pleased to see all the finishing touches added. I'm so proud of my husband. He worked hard for this. Every single detail in this club we took our time to decide on. I loved this for him. He promised that the club wouldn't have any of his street dealings. It's bad enough that the gas station had some illegal transactions. We didn't walk through the door for three minutes before Pamela came out from nowhere asking Bully to sign some paperwork.

"I'll look over it later." He took the clipboard away

from her.

"It has to be turned in today." She insisted.

"I said I'll do it myself. I don't trust you randomly telling me to sign shit."

We both walked off to the elevator to head to his office upstairs. I had to pee so bad and wanted to brush my teeth. I didn't want the stylist in my face, and I smelled like onions. I felt at peace once I was able to relieve myself. I had to pee every twenty minutes. I quickly brushed my teeth to get rid of the onion smell from my breath. Once I finished out of the bathroom, the stylist and her team arrived ten minutes later.

Quisha took her time helping me into my gown. My dress fit like a glove. She killed it with the alterations. I will wear a beautiful red gown with a long sexy slit on my thigh for the red carpet. It is very classy but also very revealing. I wanted the red-carpet pictures to look elegant. Then I will change into my next dress, which will be a silver crystal dress with red detailing. I'll be able to party comfortably in my second dress.

I have never been more satisfied than now. Since Bully and I have been married, this is the first time we can dress up like this. I'm very excited to pop out with him. Bully then changed into his suit, which is black and red. I wanted everyone to leave the office so I could fuck him right now. He looked so edible in his suit. Mmm.

"Quisha, if I weren't pregnant, Khalil would be getting me pregnant in that suit tonight!" I locked eyes with my man. I loved seeing him blush. He swore up and down real niggas don't blush, but I do something to his soul just like he does to me.

"I'm glad you two are satisfied." She giggled while adjusting Bully's suit.

There was a mental countdown in my mind. I'm so excited I didn't want to wear Bully out from it. We had a glam team doing Erin and I's makeup, hair, and nails that day. Bully, Mike, and Logic had a barber coming to the house to get them right. There was also private catering from the morning until we left later in the evening so nobody would have to worry about their appetites. I just know grand opening day will be a movie and I couldn't wait.

I had Quisha take pictures of me so I could continue to stare at it until the day came. Our fitting took about an hour. Bully did some work around the office before we left a couple of hours later. We went straight to Mike's house. I have been worrying about whatever this news is. It's unlike Erin to be able to tell me something over the phone. It obviously had to be important.

I texted her, letting her know that we were on our way. She told me to bring my appetite because she had just finished cooking dinner. I let her know I never left home without my appetite. I was ready 'cause my girl knows how to throw down in the kitchen. We made it to the house in forty-five minutes with all the traffic. Bully helped me out of the car, and we knocked on the door.

"Wassup y'all." Mike opened the door.

I hugged him before rushing past him to go to the bathroom. I had to pee again. I finished and met Erin in the kitchen. She was setting the dinner table with our plates. The aroma in the kitchen had my stomach grumbling. She made rice and peas, jerk chicken, plantains, and some type of cabbage salad. My mouth watered, looking at the beautiful plate.

"Girl, if you don't sit down and feed my God baby." She pushed me out of her way.

"You don't have to tell me twice." I meant that shit too. I sat down to eat, then Bully and Mike entered the kitchen. Everybody sat down and enjoyed the delicious food.

"Now, what happened?" I asked Erin and Mike.

"I know who's been stalking me!"

"Who? Your baby mama?" I looked at Mike.

"No, it's Edward." She said, and my mouth dropped.

"He just told me." Bully shook his head.

"Remember Mike set up my doorbell camera? Look at his ass walk to my door, but he saw the camera and left."

She pulled up the video on her app. That was indeed Edward lizard looking ass. Wow, this nigga had some nerve to stalk her and break into her condo. What is the purpose of this shit? I'm sure he thought he could get Erin back, but that's far from the truth.

"Wow, this all makes sense."

"I said the same thing. I've been looking at the camera every day, but he hasn't been back since."

"What are we going to do?" I asked.

"You two aren't going to do shit." Mike shut that down quickly. "I'ma handle it."

"That nigga has a few screws missing," I said.

"He ain't met me." Mike had an evil glare on his face. Sometimes I don't know who he or Bully is.

"Do you, you got this." I cheered him on before eating a forkful of my food.

"So, how was your honeymoon?" Erin asked, wanting to know all of the tea.

"I ate so many lobsters and fish that I think I'm good for a minute on seafood." I giggled. "It was so beautiful, though. I know it's something you two would enjoy."

"We going back." Bully chuckled. I'm sure he thought of all the sex we had on the beach.

"But what is going on with y'all two?" I asked because they were the elephant in the room.

"We're figuring it out," Erin said.

"Y'all back together. So are y'all ready to come to decorate KJ's nursery?" I asked with a smile.

"Not really." They said in unison.

"Fuck y'all. Lame ass godparents." They both laughed.

We finished our dinner and our conversation. Somehow, I convinced Bully and Mike to take me to Home Depot so I could figure out the color to paint the walls. Then Bully realized he needed a few things to put the room together. We made it a family trip, and I was excited. These days I hate to do things by myself. It just felt good to have them all around. It was always a great time.

"All the sugar daddies are in here," Erin whispered as Mike and Bully walked ahead of us.

"Some fine ones too." I agreed on the low, and we both laughed.

We located the paint department and mixed a couple of colors until I found the perfect shade of grey. I had decals to place on the wall with KJ's name and elephants that would match the aesthetic. Since we were already here, Mike wanted to knock it out and set up the nursery. I loved how they read my mind. He and Erin went home to change into more comfortable clothes, and Bully and I went home to open all the furniture boxes. They arrived about forty minutes after us. While they set up the crib and the furniture, Erin helped me wash KJ's clothes and arrange his closet. Together she and I were done in an hour doing the small things. We kicked it on my bedroom balcony while Mike and Bully continued to set up the bigger things.

"I need to know the details about y'all getting back together." I was dying to know. The last time I was in the same room with the two of them, Mike almost had a panic attack about her going on her fake date.

"It's been a lot since you have been on your honeymoon. Remember my therapist wanted Mike to join one of our sessions? I finally gave him a call and asked. He said yes, and he was there for me. We got to talk and clear the air about our problems. I got to see his point, which helped us make it work. I'm fighting for us, and he wants the same thing too."

"That sounds like a love story." They were the cutest!

"Girl, shut up."

"Seriously, I've said it since day one. Mike is crazy about you, and you are too. It was just a matter of time before y'all two figured it out. The split was only for a month."

"Yes, and that night he came home with me so we could have dinner, but as we walked through the hallway to my place, he said something was off. He went inside first to make sure everything was okay. He told me to check all my things to ensure everything was there, and my diamond earrings were missing. That's when he figured somebody broke into my place."

"I'm glad he followed his gut. We don't know how long this has been going on."

"I thought the same thing too."

"Well, congratulations on working it out with your

man. I know it was a tough time for you when it happened. I'm happy to see the smile back on your face."

We continued to talk while they finished setting up the room. It felt good to be back home. In a week, I missed out on a lot of juicy tea. I'm glad she and Mike are back together, and they figured out this stalker situation.

Chapter 10

Khalil "Bully" Wright

I couldn't hide my bright smile as I walked the red carpet to the opening of my club. Keyshia looked amazing on my side as we stopped to take pictures. My tailor-made Giorgi Armani suit fit exactly like how I wanted it to. The club was packed from wall to wall. When my limo pulled up, the line was wrapped around the building. I know we are over capacity tonight, and I just hope the police don't come to shut us down.

My private section was filled with bottles and food. I was living it up and taking it all in. I thought making it this far in the streets was hard but opening this club had to be more challenging. I wanted to say fuck it and throw in the towel so many times, but Keyshia encouraged me to keep going. I'm glad I did, though.

My DJ had everyone in the club turnt as fuck. I didn't see anyone not dancing. Keyshia had already changed into her second dress, and she hadn't stopped dancing since. I wanted her to sit her ass down somewhere so she could relax, but she's been more turnt than me. As long as she was happy, I wanted her to enjoy herself.

"The whole city came out tonight!" Mike said and

shook my shoulders roughly. This nigga was drunk.

"This shit crazy as fuck."

We stood on the balcony and watched all the partygoers. One thing I was pleased with was my security team. I didn't want my nightclub to be the hood meet up spot. If a nigga ain't from my crew, he cannot bring a pistol in this motherfucka, and I meant that shit. There was no paying extra or tryna sneak that shit in. I don't want any altercations happening here that would make the police wanna investigate shit. Even though the business is running clean, my personal shit isn't. I didn't need the FBI looking into my life.

I excused myself from the section and went to work. As the owner, I had to show my face and greet some people who cashed out for the VIP sections. There were basketball and football players, rappers, and big social media influencers in here tonight. I wanted all of them to post on social media showing their fans what a great night they were having. I went into the stock room to check on the liquor. We weren't running out, but my staff had to work fast to restock the bar. I caught Pamela sitting in the corner, being sneaky.

"What you doing in here hiding?" She jumped up when I asked.

"I was just taking a break."

"Hurry up and get your ass back to work." She went and did as I said.

"Boss." I turned around when one of the securities called me.

"Wassup?"

"There's a woman at the door asking for you."

"What is her name? What does she want?"

"Brenda Austin. She said she is your mother-in-law,

and I wasn't sure."

"I'll go check it out. Go in my section and tell my wife I'm upstairs in my office." He nodded and went to go handle that for me.

I took a deep breath and went to the club's entrance to greet April's mother. I don't know how the fuck she found out about the club's grand opening or why she is here, but I will sure find out. As I approached the entrance, she was standing to the side, waiting for me. When she saw me, I motioned for the security to let her through.

"Boy, why haven't you been answering my calls?" She walked up and hugged me.

I escorted her upstairs to my office. I wasn't prepared to deal with this tonight, but since she's already here, I might as well clear the air. I unlocked the office, and she sat on the chair in front of my desk. I sighed before taking off my jacket and sitting down too.

"I honestly didn't know how to respond," I said truthfully.

"What is all this talk I've been hearing about you getting married and having a baby?" Her eyes looked hurt.

"I did get married, and we are expecting a son in a couple of months." I turned the picture frame around that was sitting on my desk of Keyshia and me.

"Wow." Her eyes filled with tears.

"I don't want you thinking I'm crazy, Khalil."

"I know you're not mama. It's still taking me some time to adjust to it too."

"She's beautiful."

"Thank you." I wholeheartedly smiled.

"I'm still working through this. It may have been

four years ago, but it still feels like it just happened yesterday."

"You okay, babe?" Keyshia walked into the office but stopped when she looked at April's mom. She slowly walked around the table and stood next to me.

"This is April's mother, Brenda, and this is my wife, Keyshia." I introduced the two.

Keyshia sensed the sadness and tried to be understanding. "Hi, how are you?" She walked around the table to hug her.

"I've been hearing for months now that you've found someone new. I told everybody it's just Khalil being a man and handling his needs. I didn't know you were in love and found a way to move on. I'm sad you couldn't share that with me. I am happy, though, that you got yourself together. I was really worried about you." She got up from her seat to hug me.

"You're family forever, mama. April and Olivia will always be a part of our lives. We just have to live and be happy like they would have wanted us to be."

"I know, son. I'm working on the happy part. Congratulations on the marriage and the baby. Please don't think I'm a burden."

"You could never be a burden. You two share someone so special, and I'm sure she would want you two to care for each other." Keyshia stepped in when she saw April's mom about to break down and cry.

"She sure would want that." She smiled, and they hugged again.

"Thank you for coming to see me. I'ma stop hiding from you now."

"That's what I want to hear." She wiped her tears and giggled.

"Let me walk you to your car."

I kissed Keyshia on the forehead and told her to wait in the office for me to get back. I walked Brenda out to her car, and it was quicker to leave through the back. I hugged her tightly before sending her off. Quickly I went back into the club and into my office.

"That was a lot," I said when I walked in.

"Did you know she was coming?" Keyshia asked.

"No one of the security came and got me."

"You okay, babe?" She offered me a hug.

"I'm good."

"Are you positive?"

"For real, I'm good. I didn't expect to see her, but it didn't throw my mood off."

"Well, that's good, babe."

We sat in the office for half an hour. I only did that to keep Keyshia off of her feet. She had not taken her heels off since we arrived. I know her feet hurt, but she had to look good, so she didn't mind the pain. We went back into the section and partied. We didn't stay until the club closed. I was ready to get the fuck home.

Chapter 11

Keyshia Wright

My eyes scanned the envelope I was dreading to open. Inside was my Granny's life insurance check. It was another reminder that she wasn't here with me no longer. When I was about to shed a tear, Bully entered the bedroom.

"You alright, ma?" He questioned.

"Trying to be. Granny's life insurance check came in the mail." I said, holding it up to show him.

"I have been waiting for this to come." He came and scooted me over so he could sit on the bed. I looked at him confused 'cause why would this make him excited when he has all the money in the world?

"For what?"

"I'ma take you to the bank so you can invest it. Let some of the money accrue interest, and I found this laundry mat by the gas station we gonna open for you." He looked happy.

"Now, why would I wanna do that?" I was so confused. None of this sounded fun.

"You gotta have yo' own shit. You could splurge all day off of my expense, and you know I don't care, but legally something gotta be in your name. You know all of my businesses are legit, so you gotta be too. We gonna flip this check since this is in your legal name. I'ma give you all this money back but in cash. I don't want it to trace back to me. I could be gone tomorrow. What are you gonna do? You gotta have stability figured out for you and KJ if something ever happened to me. I'd be turning in my grave if you wouldn't be able to provide a safe environment for KJ because I didn't make sure I set you straight for life."

Since I met this man, all he ever spoke about was wealth. He was deep in the streets, but when he went to jail for a year after April died, he won a civil lawsuit against the prison. Two of the guards beat him badly. Bully is intelligent, so he got his lawyer and did everything he could to secure that lawsuit. He was awarded a $750,000 settlement. He invested the money into the gas station and split the restaurant with his lawyer's brother. On paper, Bully is a stand-up guy and very legit. In the streets, he is a demon to be reckoned with.

I understood everything he was saying. I loved that he always thought about the future of our family. This street shit did provide a lot of stuff for us, but in the long haul, it's his legit business we'll be living off of. So I'm down for whatever idea he comes up with because I know he won't lose.

"So you say the laundry mat is by the gas station?" I asked.

"Down the street. We can hire Hispanics to run the day to day, and we pop up here and there. Easy money. Run it for a year, and then you open a second one. You gotta come up with a business name so you can apply for a business license."

"Val's Wash Express!" I was so excited when I said it. I wanted to honor Granny by using her name.

"Granny would love that." He smiled.

"I know she would."

I was going to stay in college for Business, but once I found out about Granny's cancer diagnosis, I dropped out. After that, I worked in the club and had no other skills besides being pretty, knowing how to count money, and interior designing. I'm so glad Bully came up with this hustle because now I finally feel like I had something for myself.

I was starting to feel like a failure. I always had something going for myself, and I was starting to only feel like Bully's baby mama. I admired that Erin had something going for herself. I even thought about checking into school several times, but I figured it would be a waste of time since I wasn't passionate about anything like her. What she's doing is a lot of hard work and dedication that I don't have.

"I'll have my business people get you the license, and then we'll go to the bank."

"Alright."

I placed the check on the nightstand before getting up and going into KJ's nursery. I'm so thrilled that it's completed. I couldn't wait to bring my baby home. There was a pile of clothes to fold and hang, so I got started on it. Last week I ordered tons of clothes online, and yesterday, I finally worked myself up to wash all of them. Now the last thing to do is put it away.

Honestly, I would have more energy if Granny was alive. I'm still trying to pull myself out of the grieving funk. It's only been two months since we laid her to rest. I just couldn't sit around here crying all day because that'll only cause stress to my baby. KJ saved my soul in so many ways he doesn't even know it.

Once all of the clothes were put away, I went downstairs. I smiled at my beautiful Christmas tree. The gifts were wrapped beautifully under the tree, and I smiled, knowing that KJ would be here to open his presents next year. Christmas was in a couple of days, and my mood was still up and down, but at least I was trying to put a smile on my face. Regardless of my spirit, I have a lot to be grateful for, and I am focusing my energy on that. The doorbell rang, and I went to go answer it. Looking through the glass doors, I opened it seeing Logic.

"Wassup, sis?" He smiled, walking inside.

"Hey." I hugged him. "I was just making some hot chocolate. You want one?"

"You gonna put some marshmallows in it?"

"If that's what you want." I giggled.

"Hell yeah then."

Logic was funny to me, but Bully wasn't impressed. I have had so many talks with him to let release pressure off of his brother. He was young and will make mistakes. Bully just needed to be there for him. I thank God he made it out of that shooting. Since then, he's been chilling, and I see his change. He's been coming around more often and must have a girlfriend.

"I know it was your voice I was hearing." Bully entered the kitchen from the den. "You good?"

"Yeah. I came to see Keyshia."

"What you come to see my wife about?"

"Privately." Bully looked at him with an attitude, then went back into the den. These two still fought like children.

"What's up?" I questioned.

"When you got with my brother, did you feel like he was playing games?"

"Of course, I did. Look at Khalil. Why would I not think that?"

"I'm talking to this girl, and I fuck with her vibe, but we keep fighting because she thinks I'm playing games."

"I knew this was about a girl. You've been acting very different lately."

"How?" He questioned.

"You've been less careless. You haven't talked about bitches in a while, and you've been calm."

"That doesn't mean a female is behind it."

"Well, I think she likes you too, and if there's drama about whether or not you are playing games, she has already found herself liking you too deeply, and she doesn't want to get hurt. At this point, it's easier to call this whole relationship off if there's one red flag than to figure out what that feeling is for you. When I met Khalil, I instantly knew he was my type, and our vibe was unmatched, but how he carried himself, I didn't believe that he was single. It was always in the back of my mind that he was playing me. You know when you know is honestly all I can say. I knew from the jump I wanted to be with your brother. Other people probably thought we were rushing it, but we both felt the same way about each other. I love him, and I'm not going anywhere."

"I don't wanna say I love her yet, but I fuck with her personality and company around me."

"I wanna meet her." I sipped my hot chocolate.

"Hold on, she FaceTiming right now." He looked happy that she was calling. That boy is sprung, and he doesn't wanna admit it.

"Wassup." His voice changed and everything. I couldn't help but laugh, and he tried to shush me.

"Who's that?" She reminded me of myself when I started talking to Bully. Let me have heard one female voice. I would have been on my way to fight anyone around, and bust Bully's head 'til the white meat showed.

"My sister."

I took that as my opening to step in the camera and talk because he was acting slow as hell. I was very impressed seeing how beautiful she is. I ended up taking over, and seeing how shy he was made me smile. Logic just wanted to find love, but he thought he had to be tough to impress girls. I wanted to help him ease her mind.

"We're having brunch on Christmas Eve. You should come with Logic." I suggested.

"That would be nice." She smiled.

Logic looked at me as if he wanted to choke me. He quickly got her off of the phone.

"Why would you invite her?"

"Look, just let her come and see how she blends in, then you'll know if you like her or wanna drop her. We're opening gifts at the brunch, so buy her something like a cheap Gucci bag. You don't want to make her feel left out."

"If this shit backfires, I blame you."

"It won't backfire. You'll know what to do."

"Help me order her gift. Is it going to be here on time?"

"It should be," I said before grabbing his phone and looking for a purse for him to buy. We instantly found a cheap Gucci bag. It will be delivered to my house tomorrow, and I'll wrap it for him.

"You ain't cook anything? I'm hungry as fuck."

"Nigga, did you really ask me that? You aren't my man."

"I am your brother-in-law. You have to feed me too. Bully came with baggage, and I'm one of them."

"No, I didn't cook, but I was about to order pizza and lay up under my man."

"Well, make room for me too."

I shook my head, and we walked down to the den to join Bully. I sat on the couch and ordered our pizza. It was a cool night, and I felt the love in the room even though we weren't doing anything. Bully and Logic were taking turns playing Grand Theft Auto. I felt like I was a part of a family, and it made me feel good inside. It has always been me, Granny, and Erin. It's just nice to expand my family.

I looked at the assortments of food the Chef cooked for our brunch. My house smelled amazing, and I knew all of our family would enjoy it. I told everybody to be on time because I didn't want the food sitting here getting cold waiting for their late asses. Holidays were a big deal for me. After my mama died, Granny showed up and showed out every year so I wouldn't feel left out. At first, I was hurt, obviously, but my pain started to fade away. This Christmas was painful without her, but I am smiling while holding all of our memories close to my heart.

"Chef, this smells amazing." My stomach was already growling.

"You want me to make you a little plate?" He asked.

"I was tryna wait for everybody but fuck it. I'm

pregnant." I giggled.

Chef made me a small plate of two lamb chops with macaroni and cheese. I did need something on my stomach right away. Whenever I didn't eat fast enough, KJ made me feel nauseous. I saw Bully sneaking in and placing some gifts under the tree. I don't know where he had them hidden this whole time. This motherfucka was sneaky. I finished devouring my lamb chops.

"Thank you, Chef!" I said, washing my hands.

"Anytime, Mrs. Wright." When I was exiting the kitchen, the doorbell rang. Checking the time on my watch, our guests started to arrive on time.

"Come in." I kept the door open for Bully's mama.

"Khalil!" I yelled from the foyer so he could help her with the gifts.

"Wassup, mama." He came running in to assist her.

She hugged and kissed both of us before rubbing my belly. Once all of her gifts were placed under the tree, Logic and his date arrived. Everybody's eyes shifted to the beauty on his arm.

"This is my family." He said so we could stop staring so hard.

"Hello, beautiful! Nice to finally meet you." I welcomed her since everybody was acting like she had two heads.

"Nice to meet you. Breana." She told me her name.

"Make yourself at home. There are cocktails in the kitchen." I told her.

Breana had to be the same height as me. Her beautiful bronze skin was glowing. Whatever her skin care regiment is, it's on point. Her silky weave flowed down her back, and I loved the Bottega dress she wore. She had style, and just from her presence, I could see why

Logic wanted advice on dating her. She didn't seem like the typical airhead he fucks. Breana appears to have her shit together, and I love that.

"Since when did he get a girlfriend?" Lori, my mother-in-law, asked.

"Not sure, but he's serious about her, so we should get to know her. I think he's changing and slowing down. He for sure has matured since the incident. I gotta give him some credit." I wanted to be on Logic's side. Both Lori and Bully are always hard on him. He needed someone to have his back too.

"That's good for him." She smiled, and I could see her attitude ease.

I watched Logic and Breana in the kitchen enjoying themselves. They honestly really looked cute together. Since I have known him, I have never seen him smile this hard. Maybe love really bit him in the ass. I'm praying this works out for him. While adjusting my Granny's ornament on the tree, Mike, Erin, and Kiki arrived. They looked like a beautiful family. I loved this for her.

"You guys look so beautiful as a family." I smiled.

Erin blushed, and Mike pulled her tight. "Merry Christmas sis love you to death." She hugged me tightly. "How are you holding up today?"

"I'm hanging in there, but I am happy to have all of you guys here with me." I smiled wholeheartedly.

She looked at the tree and kissed Granny's ornament. When Granny passed, it didn't only affect me. It tore Erin down as well. Granny was also a significant role in her life as much as mine. I was the only biological grandchild, and Erin was her second out of love. When she learned about Erin being molested, she ensured Erin would be safe with us. When we got older, she told Erin and me that she would have adopted her legally, but she didn't have the means to do it. She wouldn't have qualified as an adoptive parent, but she kept close contact with Erin's adoptive mother so she could be with us all the time.

"I miss you, Gran."

"I'm sure she misses us both." I smiled.

"Auntie Keyshia, I got KJ a Christmas gift." Kiki approached me.

"Aww, that's so sweet of you, Kiki." She and KJ will be inseparable.

Mike and Bully were still loading the gifts from his car. He brought all of Kiki's gifts since she will spend Christmas day with her mother tomorrow. I loved that we could all come together today and celebrate as a family. I needed them.

"Come on, y'all, let's eat," I told everybody.

Once everybody got their plates, I ate in the kitchen with Erin. I called Breana over so we could get to know her. I couldn't wait to talk to her and get to know her personally.

"You have such a beautiful house, Keyshia," Breana said, taking a bite of her food.

"Thank you, love. What do you do?" I asked.

"I'm an esthetician. I'm certified to wax and do eyelash extensions."

"Wow, that's great. I'ma have to get my lashes done!"

I loved that she had something going for herself. I can see and hear the confidence in how she speaks and walk. I learned that she is the same age as Logic, and they've been dating for a couple of months but just took the relationship seriously.

"I'm still learning him, honestly. We are taking it slow, but I want to see what the future holds for us." She said.

"That's good for you 'cause Logic is insane!" I nudged Erin 'cause now why the fuck would she say that?

"He's not insane. He's just misunderstood. He's finding his own identity." I defended him.

"Girl, he is fucking coo-coo for cocoa puffs," Erin said, and she was dead serious too.

Breana sipped her cocktail, and I could see her wondering what she got herself into. We finished our food and our conversation so we could open our presents. I couldn't wait to see what Bully had gotten me because he has been very sneaky lately.

Bully's mama handed everybody a box with their name, and at the same time, we all opened our gifts. I received a beautiful Balenciaga handbag from Erin. We each had about forty boxes of gifts, so it took us a long time to unwrap everything.

"Aww." Immediately tears flowed down my cheeks.

"What is it?" Everybody asked.

I held up a VVS diamond heart charm that had the last picture taken of me, my mama, and Granny together when I was ten. It was so beautiful and the best gift I have ever received. The diamonds shined bright, just like my giant smile in the picture. I got up and hugged Bully so tight. I couldn't stop crying. He helped me put on my chain, and it was undeniably beautiful.

"Thank you so much, babe." I held on to him as tight as I could.

"I know you would love it."

"Best gift in the whole wide world." I smiled.

I didn't care to open the other gifts after receiving

my chain. No other gift could beat this one. When everybody finished opening their presents, Bully placed a blindfold on me, and Mike did the same to Erin. I don't know what the special surprise was, but it had to be something big.

"Walk slow, babe. You know I'm not going to let you fall." Bully said, leading me somewhere.

I slowly took my steps until I felt the wind outside. I heard everybody talking.

"What is it?" I felt giddy inside.

"For real, why am I blindfolded?" Erin asked.

"Damn, y'all can't be patient for shit," Mike told us.

We waited a few more minutes, and then they told us to remove the blindfold. My mouth dropped seeing Bully stand in front of a white G-class Mercedes Benz. I've always mentioned this being my dream car! The big red ribbon on the car made it even more beautiful. I don't know where the fuck he had it hidden because I have not seen this parked on our street. He held up the key fob for me to grab.

"I promise I don't need anything else ever again!" I lied, truly. He spoils me so he'll buy me something new again.

"It's your world, babe."

I rushed to check out my new car. Inside was KJ's car seat already installed. The red interior was beautiful, and my name was stitched into the seats. When I was done, I walked over to Erin's new truck. She had been talking about trading in her BMW for a Lamborghini Urus like Mike's but in a different color. He upgraded her to the newest make of the truck and in her favorite color, yellow. She was on cloud nine, and so was I.

Chapter 12

Kameron "Logic" Wright

I inhaled the Dior cologne I sprayed over my outfit. Looking in the mirror, I looked fresh as fuck. The last thing I put on was my Richard Millie watch and tucked my pistol in my waist. I'm taking Breana to dinner and then to the club for her birthday. Since we went to Bully and Keyshia's house last week for Christmas, we moved to the next level in our relationship.

"Kam, which earring do you like?" She asked, showing me two different pairs.

"That one." I pointed to a sparkly pair.

"I was thinking this one too." She smiled.

She had on this short ass silk dress. If she moved too fast, I saw the bottom of her cheeks peek through. My dick was instantly hard. I waited for her to finish getting dressed. Bre has been staying over at my house for weeks. She lived at home with her mom and planned to move out independently. I liked her here, though. She was cool as fuck, and we could lay up all day without a problem.

Tonight's dinner is at Ocean Prime with all of her closest friends. She wanted a dinner party and to go to the club, so I made it happen for her. Bully gave me a section at the club, and since it's one of the most popping clubs in the city, it's a plus for us.

"Alright, let's go." She walked in front of me, posing.

"They gonna have to wait a minute." I kissed her neck.

"Wait 'til later." She giggled, trying to break loose from my grip.

"You're lucky it's your birthday because you'd be back in the room right now."

"Boy, whatever." She giggled.

We walked downstairs to the driver I had for the night. Once we slid into the backseat of the Escalade, she texted all of her homegirls, letting them know we were on our way. I loved to see the smile on her face. She looked happy inside and out.

"Thank you, babe." She leaned over and kissed me with her glossy lips.

"I'm tryna show you how serious I am about you, Bre."

When I first met Breana, it was before the shooting, so I was wilding out. She wasn't having any of that, so she wasn't fucking with me anymore. Then I saw her at the mall, and we talked. I took her out a couple of times, and we decided to give it a try, but she was on my head with twenty-one questions about females. I'm not talking to anybody but her right now. Ever since I got set up, I stepped back from the bitches.

"I ain't gon' lie. You've been applying pressure." She smirked.

"You met my family, and that gotta mean something."

"It does mean a lot, Kam. Keyshia even made a lash appointment with me for New Years. I believe you now but give me the benefit of the doubt. You were on some wild shit a couple of months back, and you know I don't play none of that. If the point is to fuck on me and play games, the door is wide open for you to leave and play that game with a bird 'cause it's not me."

"Nobody is playing with you, Bre."

"I know. We have an understanding now, and the feeling is mutual." She pecked my lips.

This girl gave me a hard time. She had her shit together, and she wasn't tolerating my bullshit. All the bitches I used to talk to didn't give a fuck. I could do whatever I wanted to do to them because they wanted bragging rights. Not Breana; she doesn't give a fuck about that.

I helped her out of the truck when we made it to the restaurant. We had a private room in the back set up. She was excited as we walked through the restaurant to her room. All her friends were standing up, waiting to greet her. She looked happy and seeing her smile made me know I did my job correctly for tonight.

I just kicked back while she enjoyed her dinner with her friends. I said a few words here and there, but her friends weren't my people. I already know how insecure she is about my bullshit, so I wasn't trying to speak to anybody but her. I didn't feel like hearing her going crazy about me taking a liking to anyone in particular.

My mom sent me a text to wish Bre a happy birthday for her. That felt good that she started to acknowledge me as one of her sons and not a fuck up. I always felt like she didn't like me because she always compared me to Bully, but she didn't understand what it was like being in my shoes. I feel like we've been working on our relationship. Keyshia told me she talked to my mom to get her to ease off of me. I don't know if it'll work, but that's just how my mama is.

We left the restaurant and went straight to the club. I had fun because all my people were here too and I didn't have to stay quiet because all her friends were around. We had so much liquor in the section and smoked all the weed we brought. It was a good time.

"Happy birthday, sexy." I pulled Bre in for a kiss.

"Thank you, babe."

We both were drunk and high as fuck. We partied until three in the morning. When we returned to my apartment, we fucked until the sun came up. I don't know what the fuck we were doing, but we had a good time tonight.

I woke up the next afternoon and didn't even hear Bre get out of bed. She got up and left to go to work early. I don't know how she had the strength to do it 'cause I was hungover as fuck. I got up and went into the bathroom to brush my teeth before I showered and started my day. I didn't have shit to do, so I was gonna stop at Bully's crib first. He's usually home around this time.

I was rushing to get out of the house. I hated being home alone. That's why I was always in the streets. Everybody around me had a girl or someone to come home to. I had nobody; that's why I fucked with so many females. When I got in my car, I sped to Bully's house. I was there in fifteen minutes. I parked my car next to Keyshia's G-Wagon. I got out to ring the doorbell.

"I didn't know you were coming by today." Keyshia opened the door.

"I didn't think I was either, but I had nothing else to do."

"How was Bre's birthday last night? You guys

looked like y'all had fun." She referred to our Instagram stories.

"That shit was hella fun."

"Glad you guys enjoyed yourselves."

"Where Bully at?"

"Getting ready to leave. Don't nobody come and hang out with me."

"You want a friend Keysh?"

"I do, actually, but you're being mean, so fuck you too." She threw her middle finger at me. Her hormones were always on ten.

"Why the fuck is my wife cussing you out?" Bully asked, coming down the stairs.

"She's an emotional mess. Control your girl."

"I'm not a mess. You all be leaving me because I'm pregnant and can't do anything."

"What you want to do then, Keyshia?"

"I wanna shop on Rodeo Drive and go out to lunch."

"Come on then." I'll hang out with her. We usually had a good time, and she didn't nag like Bully.

"You for real?" She looked surprised.

"What am I gonna lie for? I ain't got shit else to do either."

"Let me go get dressed." She rushed up the stairs.

"You gonna be out shopping all day." Bully chuckled while looking in the refrigerator.

"I really ain't got shit else to do." I shrugged.

"You been good though, lil' bro?" He asked.

"I been straight. Just tryna stay out the way."

"You think you could handle stepping it up some more?"

"What do you mean?" I asked.

"I'ma do count this weekend. I need an extra

person."

This was big news to me. Whenever Bully and Mike did count, I wasn't even allowed to be around 'cause they thought I was a distraction. I don't know where the fuck Mike will be at for him to not be available for this. When it comes to the big shit, Bully never reaches out for my help.

"I can do it, but where's Mike?"

"We just need to rotate. I been tryna catch up with a lot of work since he handled the business while I was busy opening up the club."

"I'm down for it." I smiled, and he did too.

I guess I've been proving myself to them. Living in their shadows is hard as fuck. Niggas expect me to be as turnt and crazy as them because they're my brothers. Bully and Mike are legends in these LA streets. These niggas make shit happen, no matter how big or small. Every bitch wanna fuck them, and every nigga will do whatever just to hang in the crew. A lot of eyes and expectations are on me, and they don't even see that. They notice when I wild out, but not that I'm trying to build my own legacy.

Keyshia returned after thirty minutes of her getting dressed. She was happy to go on this shopping trip. Bully had left out fifteen minutes earlier. We left their house in her G-Wagon. She thought she was the queen because she tossed her keys for me to drive.

"How the fuck does your man own a gas station and your tank stay on E?" I asked when I started the truck.

"Look, mind ya' business." She laughed.

I shook my head and drove off to the gas station. I really don't understand how she doesn't have any gas in her car. It's like a barber never having a fresh cut. It just doesn't make sense. I parked at one of the pumps and went to tell the attendant to fill the tank while Keyshia went inside to grab herself some snacks.

"Grab me some hot fries and an Arizona too." She was greedy and wasn't thinking of my needs either.

I walked outside and saw the niggas that was supposed to be paying attention to the gas station staring Keyshia down. Everybody around knows Keyshia by now and not to even look her way. They were all playing with their lives, and because she's my sister, I stepped in and did what Bully would have done. I walked up to the main nigga lusting after her and punched him in his face. I hit hard as a motherfucka 'cause he fell to the ground after one punch.

"Fuck you niggas staring at my sister for? Y'all wouldn't even move your eyes had Bully been standing here." I was hot!

"My bad, Logic. It wasn't even like that." One of the other niggas said.

"Did I tell you to speak to me nigga?" I dropped him too with one punch.

I turned around, and Keyshia looked shocked. I don't know what her ass was surprised about. She knows damn well Bully would have done the same. She should be used to this shit by now. I helped her get in the passenger seat while I finished pumping the gas. She was on the phone with Bully when I got in the car.

"Those niggas are still sleeping on the ground, Khalil." She was giggling and shit, but she was shocked just a few seconds ago.

"I'm about to head up there now. Niggas do buster shit when I'm not around. Good looking, bro. These niggas gonna catch a bullet." He hung up the phone. He sounded pissed. I would be too.

"You didn't have to do all of that," Keyshia said as she ate her Skittles.

"It's about respect. Had I not checked them niggas the next time you come around, one of them might speak to you. Bully doesn't play that shit, and I wouldn't either. If he's not around, these niggas are supposed to have the same respect when they see you."

"I understand when you put it like that."

I drove to Rodeo Drive so we could shop. I still wanted to buy Bre some more shit even though her birthday was yesterday. We went into every store and left with something. I gotta go shopping with Keyshia more often. She and I had similar taste, and it killed time until Bre was off work, especially since I had nothing to do.

Chapter 13

Erin Jackson

I couldn't be any more excited to finish my long day of school and get in my bed to relax for the rest of the day. Today was Wednesday, and I didn't have to be at the club until Friday afternoon, so I was excited about my little break. Quickly I replied to Keyshia's text before sliding it back into my purse. I hit the alarm on my key fob and got into my car. I haven't driven the new Lamborghini Mike gifted me for Christmas yet. He said there were more customizations he wanted to add to the truck, so I had to wait another week. Until then, my BMW was perfectly fine to drive around in. I turned on my music and immediately felt the cold steel of a gun hit the back of my head. My heart instantly dropped to the pit of my stomach.

"Bitch you thought you would move on and be happy without me?" Edward's familiar angry voice filled the car.

For some odd reason knowing it was Edward made me feel slightly better. Not all the way, but just a little better. I know his weak points. He was my man for years. If anything, I know for sure I am tougher than this nigga because I am smarter than him. He doesn't use his brain, and that's why he always gets caught up because he acts on emotions nine times out of ten. I looked in my rear-view mirror and saw his ski mask pulled over his face. We locked eyes, and my heart felt nothing. I knew he would return soon since Mike and I caught him on my Ring camera, but I didn't think it would be this way.

"W-what are you talking about?" I stuttered.

"Got all my niggas telling me about you parading this nigga around the city."

He showed me a picture on my Instagram of Mike and me kissing. It was a good picture of us too. We both looked happy.

"What do you want with me?" I asked 'cause now I was tired of playing this game with him.

"Drive!" He shouted, never releasing the gun from the back of my head.

I did as he said because he looked like a maniac. I drove out of the parking lot and kept my eyes on him. I didn't know what the fuck he thought was going to happen, but it won't end well on his end. I'ma use all my strength to make sure I make it back to my family.

"Pull into that lot." He instructed.

It was an empty parking lot. My heart dropped. I did as he said. When I pulled in, he got out of the backseat and snatched open my door with his gun still on me. He opened my trunk and told me to get in. I wanted to fight right here, but I knew it wasn't a bright idea with a gun pointed in my face. He saw how hesitant I was and pushed me inside of the trunk. I fell inside pretty hard, but that was the least of my worries.

I patted my nurse uniform and forgot my phone was in my purse. I lifted my sleeve and used my Apple watch to text Mike. My phone had a passcode on it, and it was on silent in my purse so that Edward wouldn't know. I tried as quickly as I could to text him for help.

He drove for about five minutes, and when the car stopped, I assumed we were at a red light. I used the trunk release button from the inside of the trunk to pop it open. If it doesn't work, I'll just have to kick out the taillights with my tennis shoes. Once I saw the light outside, I knew we were at an intersection. I jumped out as fast as possible and screamed while I ran. I saw some of the drivers' mouths dropped that were behind my car. I ran to the gas station that was on the corner and saw Edward get out of my car and run in the opposite direction. He left my car in the middle of the intersection, and I was scared to go back. I'm not sure if there's a tracker in there or not. His dumb ass could have left an explosive. I used my apple watch to call Mike, but since I was so far away from my phone, it didn't connect.

"Excuse me, can I use your phone?" I asked the gas station attendant. He's one of the bystanders that saw it all unfold.

"Yes, ma'am." He handed me his unlocked phone.

I dialed Mike right away. Fuck 911. The phone rang, and he didn't answer. I called again, and he picked up the second time.

"Baby." I cried when I heard his voice. I felt relieved.

"Where the fuck you at?" His voice sounded angry.

"I'm at a gas station. Umm, what street is this?" I asked the attendant.

Once I gave Mike my direct location, he told me he was on his way and to wait in the gas station. I did as he said. Knowing the people in this area, I'm sure the police were already called. Not even seconds after Mike hung up; I heard the police sirens. I wiped my tears and waited for

Mike. I could see out of the window the police officers were looking for me, but I was not moving.

I felt relief when I saw Mike's Escalade pull up, then Keyshia's G-Wagon behind his. Mike, Keyshia, and Bully rushed into the gas station to find me. I melted in his arms and couldn't hold back the tears anymore. I was scared as fuck, but the thought of losing the people I loved the most disturbed me.

He hugged me and reassured me I would be okay. "Don't tell the police it was him. Say it was a carjacking or robbery story." He whispered in my ear.

"Okay." I knew he wanted to handle it personally.

We left the gas station and crossed the intersection to where my car and the police were. I was still shaken up, and the police saw it. They asked so many questions, but I did as Mike instructed.

"I just got out of class, sir. I got in my car and got ready to drive off, and the person was already in my car. He had a gun and a ski mask, so I have no idea what he looked like. He told me to drive off, and then he told me to drive into a parking lot that was empty by my school. He forced me into the trunk, and once I felt the car stop moving, I used the emergency trunk release. I just ran and didn't look back. I don't know anything else."

My story was very credible. I live in Los Angeles, and carjacking luxury vehicles is an everyday thing out here. We went to my car to see if anything was missing from my purse. My phone was there and all of my money. He didn't take anything. He must have just ran when I got out of the trunk. He wasn't the most competent criminal. That's why I knew I could outsmart him in some way.

The officer gave me his card and told me he would investigate this. I nodded and tried to get them away since I knew Mike would make sure Edward didn't bother me again. First, this nigga broke into my condo, and now he was in my car trying to do God knows what had me shook. He is getting more reckless and closer to me.

"I'm so sorry this happened to you." Keyshia hugged me.

"I can't believe this shit, man."

"I'm so glad you didn't freeze and used your brain. The second Mike got the text we were in the car trying to find you since we knew you were last at school."

"Thank this Apple watch." I tried to have some humor in this fucked up situation.

"You are coming home with me. They will do what they gotta do, but you need to be safe at home with me."

I watched as Bully tried to calm Mike, but he was upset. Bully drove my car to his gas station to park. Mike said he needed it left in a safe public location just in case Edward put a tracker in it. They needed to make sure it was safe for me before I could drive it again. I put all of my stuff in Keyshia's truck since I was going home with her. Mike took me to our house first to get some clothes, and Keyshia followed behind.

"I love you so much, E." Mike squeezed my thigh as he drove. "I promise you I'ma find this nigga."

"He is following me at this point. How did he find me at school of all places?"

"He's been watching you. Look, you don't have to worry. I'ma escort you inside to grab a couple of things, and we got somebody watching Bully's crib so you and Keyshia will be safe inside."

"Alright." I sighed.

I just wanted to relax today, but this hiked up my blood pressure. We soon arrived at our home, and he helped me out of the car and then helped Keyshia out of her truck. I went upstairs and started grabbing clothes and all of my beauty products. I even packed a couple of things for Mike. I was in and out in twenty minutes. He followed Keyshia to their house, where a car was sitting in their driveway. He went to make sure he knew who it was before he told Keyshia it was safe to park in the garage. Bully had pulled up at the same time as us with Logic in his car.

"You feeling a little better?" Bully asked before hugging me.

"Of course, now that I am safe with family."

"Logic is going to take y'all to get some food and whatever essentials y'all need. Keysh, you might as well order a bunch of food so y'all both can kick back. Y'all are safe with him, and let him drive the truck, Keysh. You need to get off of your feet, bae. He's going to drop y'all back home, and Winston will stay here and monitor the house. This is the safest place for you to be, Erin." Bully said.

"Alright."

"You can breathe now, sis." He tried to reassure me everything was okay.

Mike took my suitcase out of his car and my purse from Keyshia's truck to place in the guest bedroom. Once he was done, we got in Keyshia's truck, and Logic drove us to Wingstop. Keyshia ordered us a party platter since Bully told her to. She said she had stocked groceries, so we didn't need to stop anywhere else. I didn't care about the food; I was relieved I got away from that dumb ass nigga. My mind was so confused. This nigga did me so dirty, but he was mad that I happily moved on. Jealousy is so dangerous.

"It's going to be okay," Keyshia said, knowing I was still worrying.

"This is just ridiculous."

"They'll handle it like they always do." She said, referring to Mike and Bully.

"I'm sure they will." That's one thing I am confident in. "Can we change the conversation? I don't wanna talk about it anymore. Logic, how are you and Bre doing?"

"We good for now." He casually said.

"Ooh, look! I got my eyelashes done by her last week." Keyshia blinked a couple of times for me to see Breana's work.

"She did a great job. I'm going to have to book with her too."

Keyshia said our food was ready, so we all went inside to pick it up. Logic carried the food tray, and I had the bag with the fries and condiments. I couldn't wait to return to the house to shower and see what was going on with Mike. It made me nervous that he was possibly out there doing something to get caught up. I hope he's paying attention and can safely execute this.

As we were in the truck, I texted Mike, but he didn't respond. Knowing him, he had his phone turned off. When we made it to the house, I went straight upstairs to the guest bedroom to unpack my suitcase. On the nightstand, Mike left his phone. I gathered my clothes and soap to take my shower. Thank God there was a bathroom in the bedroom. I slipped my braids into my bonnet before turning on the hot water. Quickly I wiped off my makeup and cleansed my face before getting in the shower.

I tried to relax, but my mind went everywhere. I didn't feel at ease since I couldn't contact Mike. Trying my hardest to brush everything off, I finished scrubbing myself and washed off before exiting. I went into the bedroom and dried off before changing into a crop top and leggings. I lay on the bed for a while before Keyshia came into the room with a plate of food in her hand for me.

"I brought you some food." She laid the plate on the nightstand.

"Thanks."

"Are you still worried?" She asked.

"I can't get in touch with Mike. He left his phone."

"Girl, call his burner." She said like it was nothing.

"I don't have his burner."

"Let me get my phone." She left the room for about a minute before she came back in with a black flip phone.

"Why the hell do you have a flip phone?"

"I don't leave without it. I can call Bully in any emergency. He gave me this when Logic was shot."

"Whatever. Can you call you Mike?"

"Yeah."

She opened the phone and dialed Bully's burner number. I shook my head when she started to blush. This wasn't the time for that. These two could make you sick.

"Oh yeah, Erin wants to talk to Mike. She doesn't have a burner to call him." She told Bully. "Here." She handed me the phone before exiting the room.

"Wassup, babe?" Mike said when he got on the phone. I felt myself calm down.

"You left your phone, and I was getting worried."

"I left it on purpose. I'm good, ma. We got him already."

"We could say that over the phone?" He was talking too freely.

"We on the burner. I had my niggas hunt his stupid ass down. I paid a lot of money to catch this nigga."

"Is he dead yet?"

"Nah, he just passed out. We were just having some fun first." He chuckled, and I know it was vicious shit going on over there, and I didn't want to know the details.

"That doesn't sound safe." I giggled a little. "Alright, I feel better now since talking to you. Please continue to be safe and make it back home to me, babe."

"I'ma always make it back home to you."

"I believe you." I truly did.

We hung up, and I felt better instantly. I turned on the TV in the room and watched shows I'd never seen before. Keyshia came back into the room with me an hour later. She looked like she had showered too and changed into comfortable clothes. We both lay on the bed and ate snacks.

"What time are they coming home?" I said, noticing it was getting later and later.

"Probably a couple more hours or in the morning."

I started to get antsy again, but I knew there wasn't any reason to be. I couldn't lay here forever, so I got up and told Keyshia we should finish KJ's nursery. The room was decorated and completed, but tons of clothes still needed to be washed and folded. This little boy had more clothes than me. I popped off the tags to the clothes Keyshia had in a corner, then loaded them into the washer with the baby detergent. I went back into the room and started to hang clothes up.

"I'm starting to want my own baby now," I admitted.

"Wow, that's a big step for you."

"Therapy has been working for me."

"You have been a lot happier."

"I just feel new again. I'm not going to lie. This whole thing with Edward made me feel like I was cursed. I had to breathe and remind myself that I earned this happiness."

"You sure did earn this. Your whole life did a three-sixty change."

"I just want better for myself. Before this happened, I talked to Mike about selling the condo, and we're working on buying a house."

"That's good for you two. I'm sure Mike is excited." She giggled.

"He is, and hopefully, baby Simmons will be conceived after that."

"That man wants to put a baby inside of you so bad."

"Since the very first day we fucked." I laughed.

"Man, things have really come full circle for us."

"It sure has. You are married and a mom now. I finally conquered the trauma and demons which allowed me to love Mike."

Instantly I smiled because my heart became warm, and I started to blush. The love that filled my heart wouldn't be possible without Mike pushing me to want better for myself. He didn't come in my life to boss me around me like these niggas nowadays. He came to elevate me, and I'd do anything that man needs because I know he has my back.

We finished hanging and folding clothes. With the amount of shit baby KJ has, there isn't a point to even have a baby shower. By midnight I was ready to lay down and go to sleep. Mike and Bully still haven't returned yet, but I know he will soon. I got in bed and watched TV until

I fell asleep.

Looking at the clock on the nightstand, I felt Mike slide into the bed behind me around 3 am. He had showered and changed into the clothes I packed. I wrapped my arms around him, and we cuddled tightly. Being in his presence, I felt so safe that I started to cry. I've been holding in so much, and the people who hurt me in my life seemed to keep resurfacing. This situation with Edward could have been worse, but it's all over now. I can breathe now. I never have to think about that man ever again.

"Thank you." I cried softly.

"I got you forever, ma. I don't give a fuck who it is. Nobody is going to play with you."

"I love you."

"I love you on my soul." I know he meant it.

I am no longer accessible to my abusers. I have elevated so far in my life that they cannot touch me or be a constant thought in my mind. I feel the safest I have ever felt in my whole life. I am now free of all pain, guilt, and harm. I shall continue to live my life peacefully and freely.

Chapter 14

Michael "Mike" Simmons

A week has passed since Erin escaped her death trap by that lame ass nigga. I know my woman well enough to know that she isn't alright, like she says. Every day her mouth tells me not to worry about her, but I see her anxiety and how fidgety she has become. The worse is behind her now, and there isn't a need for her to worry any longer. Just to be on the safe side, I've been dropping her off at school the last couple of days and picking her up. If it eases her anxiety, it makes me happy.

I sat in my truck parked near the entrance of her class. She would be done in a couple of minutes, but I needed her input on an investment I'm thinking about. My uncle owned a barbershop in the nineties, but it has since fallen off. He asked me to step in and take over financially so we could keep the business in the family. At first, I didn't want any parts of it, but I did some thinking and realized it's something I should do just to keep a legal paper trail.

Once I saw Erin approaching the truck, I greeted her and opened her door. She always looked good in her uniform to me. Her achieving her goals made me attracted to her ten times harder.

"You good, ma?" I asked when I got back in the car.

"I'm amazing now that I'm with you." She leaned over to kiss me.

"Me too, bae."

I drove off and headed to the barbershop. We couldn't stay too long anyways. I had to pick Kiki up from her mama's house. Tonight is Keyshia's birthday dinner at their house. I know Erin, and I wouldn't hear the last of it if we were late. Once I got to the barbershop, I parked in front of the door. I watched my uncle inside as he cleaned clippers.

"What are we doing here?" Erin asked, confused.

"You'll see in a second, bae."

We walked in, and Erin and uncle Ronnie immediately hugged. He has been around a few times since I've been with Erin and has told me how he thinks Erin is the one for me. I wouldn't have just anybody around my girl or daughter if I didn't trust them. I didn't fuck with too many of my family, but Ronnie is a cool nigga. He stuck around when my dad left. He took on the role and stepped up as a father figure before he had his own kids.

"Nice to see you again." Erin smiled.

"What do you think about the place?" He asked.

"It needs a lot of work, but I wanna do it." Something just felt right.

This place is a significant childhood memory for me. I came to this barbershop every week for a fresh cut and to hang out with my uncle. I couldn't let him sell this place, especially now since the price to own a business on Melrose is sky high. It's a lot of competition on this street, but the right amount of money could turn this into the perfect investment.

"You wanna do what?" Erin asked me.

"Ronnie was looking into selling this place. He asked me to step in and turn it around so we can keep it in the family."

"Oh, okay, that makes sense for you."

"What do you think?" I asked her.

"I would love to see you doing something positive, so that's a hell yeah for me." She smiled while finishing her sentence.

"Alright." I chuckled.

Ronnie and I finished up our conversation before leaving. I'll bring in a lawyer to get the contract side of our business started. I love my uncle, but I love my paper more. I'm not about to do shit without my end being covered first. It'll take some time for us to merge everything with my name, but once it's completed, it'll be ready for reconstruction.

You think you know and trust family, but when money gets involved, shit takes a turn sometimes. I didn't want to think Ronnie would be a nigga like that but covering my assets would be the only way I wouldn't have to find out.

"Why you didn't tell me about this beforehand?" Erin asked as I drove.

"I didn't know if I wanted to do it at first. It wasn't a big deal for me. That's why I brought you along with me. I know you would tell me the right thing."

"I don't think it would hurt for you to invest."

"Me either."

It took me a good forty-five minutes to get to Shana's house. I called Kiki ten minutes before I pulled up to tell her I was almost there. I didn't have time for Shana today, and I didn't feel like seeing her ass or hearing her voice. I parked my truck in the front and went to get my baby. Looking through the window of Shana's door, I could see her rushing to open the door, but Kiki bumped her out of the way.

"I'm ready, daddy." Kiki opened the door.

"Tell yo' mama bye first." I made her kiss her mama before leaving.

No matter how I felt about Shana, I wouldn't want her to feel left out. She's a good ass mama when it comes to our daughter. From the day Kiki was born, Shana has been hands on. I may not like her romantically, but I'm thankful for how she is raising our daughter. I was happy we were in and out. It was almost 5 pm, and we had to be at Bully and Keyshia's house by 8 pm.

"Erin, can you help me pick out something to wear?" Kiki asked when I was pulling up to our house.

"Come on; I got you." The two of them ran out of the truck, leaving me in the garage.

I shook my head and went upstairs to shower while they did their thing. I always get left out anyways. I washed up as quickly and thoroughly as possible because Erin needed time to retwist my dreads. She did them once a week. Once I was all clean, I changed into the outfit I laid out this afternoon. I wore a polo shirt from Alexander McQueen, Purple jeans, and the McQueen shoes to match. I got myself dressed while Erin went into the shower.

"Kiki, where you at?" I walked out of my bedroom to look for her.

"Don't come in. I'm getting dressed, daddy." She had her door locked.

"Excuse me, damn."

That's another reason why I couldn't wait to have another child. Kiki was too independent. She didn't need me anymore, and I missed it. I try to bond with her, but she rather be in my presence and know that daddy is one phone call away than to hang out with me like old times. I didn't become cool to her until Erin came around, and she still didn't want me around too much. She's just into girly things. I went back into my bedroom, and Erin was out of the shower already.

"That little girl just dissed me," I said 'cause my feelings were hurt. I would have waited for her to change and give her the privacy she needed, but she said it like I had to move away from her door or else she was gonna fuck me up.

"What she say?" She giggled.

"It doesn't matter. When do little girls get their periods? She acts like she already has it. Got a damn attitude like her mama."

"I'm sure she has a couple more years before she gets it. She's just a big girl now, Mike."

She finished getting herself together before I sat down so she could retwist my dreads. It took about thirty minutes since it's still neat from her last retwist. She did her makeup and curled her hair before slipping into her dress.

"You look good as fuck." Her dress looked like it was painted on her skin.

"Thank you, babe."

"All I need is five minutes with you." I was dead serious too.

"Stop playing."

"I'ma show you how serious I am."

"Go away, Mike! We gotta hurry up."

If we didn't have to leave for real, I would have gotten mine. She was ready to go a couple of minutes later. I yelled for Kiki to get in the car while I locked the doors and set the alarm on the house. It was traffic on the freeway, and I had to exit to make it on time. Their home wasn't too far away from mine. I got there in thirty minutes.

"Damn," Erin said under her breath.

Bully went all out for Keyshia's birthday. Whoever he hired to make their house look like a castle executed that shit. I parked in the driveway and helped my ladies out of the car. Their home had hundreds of lights that lit the entire block up. It didn't look like cheap Christmas lights. This shit looked like a wedding was about to take place. When I was about to knock, a man opened the door with a tray of drinks in his hands.

"Welcome to Keyshia's birthday dinner." He smiled.

"Thank you." Erin took a drink and walked in.

Bully's mom met us at the door. I always thought of her as my second mom. We had a close relationship, and she was tight as fuck with my mama too. Kiki even called her Gigi.

"Look at you guys!" She hugged all three of us.

"Hi, Gigi." Kiki pecked her cheeks.

"Hi, my baby. Go outside and play with the kids." Kiki took off and did as she said.

"Is Keyshia here yet?" Erin asked.

"No, Khalil texted me that they are on their way. He didn't want her here seeing the whole setup."

"She is going to love this." Erin smiled.

We went into the backyard to place Keyshia's presents at her gift table. I saw Logic at one of the tables talking with Jared and Donte, who are their cousins.

"Damn my nigga you got big," Donte said as I approached the table.

"That nigga is skinny. I'm bigger than him." Logic flexed his muscles that weren't there. We couldn't stop laughing.

"Good looking for getting me that info last week," I told Jared.

"You already know, bro." He nodded.

If it weren't for his people, I wouldn't have been able to get to Erin's ex so fast. Bully and I was under Jared, Donte, and Ice. If it was something we couldn't get our hands on, they usually were able to handle it somehow. I never cared to ask how since I didn't get down like that. I just know them niggas got major pull, and it's helpful when we need it. They all fell back from the streets but ran the business on the low. They left the street shit to Bully and me. We just buy our kilos from them since it's a family business. Our shit runs smooth, and we haven't had any problems.

"Your girl good?" Donte asked.

"She good for the most part. I could see she's still a little shaken up."

"That nigga was fucked up bad." Jared chuckled.

He and Donte came to the warehouse that day to make sure I got the right nigga. I tortured that motherfucka for hours. I didn't have any regrets, and everybody sat back and watched. When it comes to our family, everybody knows we are all gonna slide behind some shit.

"It was worth it." I drank my Don Julio.

Bully's mom came into the backyard and told everybody to gather in the middle because Keyshia and Bully were walking in. Erin came and stood by me. I don't know why everybody was tryna be quiet when she knew it was a surprise and that we were all here.

"Happy birthday!" We all yelled when they walked in.

"Aww." She stopped in her tracks and cried. This is a beautiful setup, though, and with her hormones, I could see why she cried.

Chapter 15

Keyshia Wright

Two months later ...

I couldn't help but feel excited when Erin pulled up in her truck. We were meeting with all the girls for a spa day, and I was happy I didn't have to drive. Being nine months pregnant, there's not much I could do by myself. She got out of the car to help me get in the passenger seat.

"Thank you, bestie!" I said before strapping on my seat belt.

"Gotta keep you and my baby safe." She drove off.

"I need this massage so desperately. Every part of my body hurts." I sighed.

"Do you see how big your belly is? I'm sure it hurts. KJ doesn't have any room to move around."

"He is getting his eviction papers! I can't wait to meet him."

"I know, it's almost time!"

"Any day now, you can come on out," I told KJ while rubbing my belly.

We listened to music and had a great conversation on the way to the spa. It was about forty minutes away from my house. When we pulled up, we checked in, and the receptionist took us into Jasmine and Kaylen's room. I had grown very close to them. Mariah was missing, but I'd catch her another day.

"Hi, ladies!" I walked in and greeted them.

"Look at you, mama." Kaylen got up to hug me.

I loved Kaylen. We both were raised by our grandmothers and dealt with the heartache of not having our moms alive. Her grandmother is still alive and around, and I honestly wished I could have the same thing. We had a very close bond, and I consider her a friend, something like a close sister.

Jasmine, on the other hand, is like Erin. She's a ride-or-die bitch, and I love her ass to death. It doesn't matter what I need. She will take care of me. I love her beautiful children also. I'm glad I could connect with these beautiful women and build a bond. They weren't haters. Once you were in with them, then there's no getting out. It's filled with genuine love and a bunch of respect for each other. I love it here!

"KJ looks like he's ready to come out." Jasmine helped me sit down.

"Girl, any day now. I just turned thirty-seven weeks, and I'm growing impatient."

We all changed into our robes and got ready for our massages. When my masseuse laid her hands on my body, I felt like I was in heaven. This prenatal massage was what my body needed. I even caught myself falling asleep here and there. After the massages, we went into another room for a facial.

"I'm craving devil eggs so bad right now." I couldn't shake my craving.

"Come with me to my house, and I'll have my chef make you some," Jasmine said, and my eyes popped open.

"That's all you had to say." I giggled.

She stopped her facial so she could text her chef. My mouth watered, thinking about how I would devour the devil eggs soon. I've been craving them since Erin picked me up earlier.

"I need my eyelashes done," Erin said, and Kaylen agreed.

"You haven't gone to Bre yet for your lashes?" I asked.

"She did my last fill, and she did her shit." Erin giggled.

"I need mine done too," Jasmine said.

"I can ask her to come to do all of our lashes if that's cool with y'all?" I suggested.

"Yeah, have her come to my house," Jasmine said.

I texted her to see if she could do four sets of lashes. For the remaining hour, we all relaxed and enjoyed the break from our family. We loved our men and children to death, but it felt good to be pampered and enjoy the quietness. Once we were done from the spa, we went to Jasmine's house. I texted Bully, letting him know I won't be done until later and if he could pick me up instead of Erin driving me back home. Of course, he told me to let him know when I was ready.

It took us some time to get to Jasmine's house. When her gate opened, I fell in love with her house all over again. She lived in a big ass mansion. I would never leave my house if I lived here. Erin came to help me get out of the truck. When we got inside, I went to use the bathroom. I had to relieve myself every thirty minutes. I was holding it in during the car ride here. I washed my hands and met them in the kitchen. They were making themselves plates since Jasmine's chef made us plenty of food.

"Here are your devil eggs." Jasmine handed me a platter of about twenty devil eggs.

"Y'all can have one each." I tried to share.

"Girl, eat them eggs. Don't nobody want that but you." Kaylen said, and we all laughed.

After I piled my plate high as a mountain with this delicious food, we went to eat in her backyard. The weather was so nice outside. I ate my devil eggs one by one until it was just the tray left.

"So tomorrow I'll come by your store Jas to get some new hair. I want my weave to be laid for labor. I'll make an appointment with you to do my hair Kaylen."

"Just text me the length and style you want, and I'll have my assistant drop it off to you. You're almost ready to pop. You don't need to be outside doing a lot."

"Thank you."

"Have your anxiety been under control?" Kaylen asked Erin.

"I'm okay now, for real. It's been a couple of months since Mike took care of it, and I'm good. I feel safe again." Erin referred to Edward kidnapping her.

"I'm so glad your mind shifted into survival mode in that situation," Jasmine said.

"I am too. You are strong as hell." I agreed.

"Well, my graduation is in a week. I am having a small celebration party, and I want you all there, of course." Erin said.

"I'm so fucking proud of you!" I cheered her on.

"Don't you feel relieved?" Jasmine asked.

"Girl, don't I? I'm so ready for this next chapter of my life. I love the pieces I'm putting together to build this beautiful woman."

"I get it. I used to be all over the place until I connected the dots with my family." Kaylen said.

"Wait, you never told me how you were able to connect with your brothers. You guys are so close I thought you were raised with them." I asked Kaylen.

"No, I didn't meet them until some years ago. I hired a private investigator to find my biological dad and his family. I found out that my father had recently passed away and that he left two sons. Donte and Jared were mean as fuck at first." She laughed. "But for right reasoning, though. We took a DNA test, and then they welcomed me. Coming into each other's lives so late, I thought it would be hard, but once we finally connected, it felt like we've known each other all of our lives."

"That's a blessing," I said.

"Do you want to find your dad?" She asked me.

"No, I don't care to look for him. My Granny said he was no good. He was abusive to my mom while she was pregnant with me."

"Damn."

We continued to enjoy each other's company before Breana texted me, alerting me that she was at the gate. Jasmine let her in. We were all excited to get our lashes done. It's funny how we all needed a fill at the same time. Bre had met Jasmine and Kaylen before at my birthday party. They took a liking to her, so that's why Jasmine was cool with her coming to her home. While Bre set up her table and equipment, I made her a small plate of the food we ate.

"Thank you, Keysh." She said when I handed it to her.

"You're welcome. How are you?" I asked.

"I'm good. How are you?"

"Just ready to look pretty."

"You always look stunning."

"I don't always feel like it. This baby took my good looks away."

"Lies." She giggled.

She ate her food before washing her hands and starting with Jasmine's lashes. I lay on the couch and dozed off. Erin woke me up when it was my turn to get my lashes done. All three of them were finished, so I must have been sleeping long. I was so tired and full. I stretched a little before lying down on the table. She was done with my lashes about forty-five minutes later.

I texted Bully to tell him to come to pick me up. I needed to shower and get in my bed, plus I was missing him already. He made it to me in an hour. I smiled, seeing his handsome self pull up and get out of his truck to get me. I kissed him so nasty because I missed him all day.

"I missed you," I admitted.

"You know I missed you more than you missed me." He said when he drove off.

"That's not even possible." I giggled.

I just laid back and continued to gaze at him while he drove home. I felt so much love I got emotional. I'm happy to be in the hands of an amazing man who wants the best for me. I couldn't wait to bring our child into the world. When we made it home, he opened the door, and I walked into a trail of roses leading up the stairs to our bedroom. The house smelled amazing. I don't know what food he had for us, but it smelled heavenly.

"Come on, baby." He led me to the balcony in our bedroom. It was beautifully decorated, and the table decor was the ultrasound pictures. My emotional ass couldn't stop crying. "Sit down." He pulled the chair out and slid off my sandals for me.

He left and came back with two champagne glasses. He poured himself Veuve Clicquot and then Sparking Apple Cider for me. I giggled because he was so thoughtful. I sipped the cider while he went to get our food. I felt like a princess. My stomach growled when he sat the plate in front of me.

"Thank you, baby. This is so beautiful, and I didn't expect this."

"We are celebrating."

"Celebrating what?"

He removed a gold box with a pink bow from his pocket and placed it on the table. I didn't know what was in a gift box we could celebrate. I opened it, and it was a set of pink keys. I still didn't understand.

"What are the keys for?" I asked.

"Your laundry mat is fully remodeled how you wanted, and it's ready to open." He smiled hard.

"Oh wow." I looked at the set of keys. "Val's Wash Express." I silently said. I named the laundry mat after Granny. My heart was overwhelmed. "Thank you for making this happen for me."

Bully is the businessman in our marriage. He handles everything. I honestly forgot about it. Months ago, he asked me a couple of questions after we deposited Granny's life insurance check into my new business account. He hasn't said anything else since then. I didn't know he was silently working on it for me with everything he had going on.

"Look." He pulled out his phone and showed me the pictures of the place. I balled my eyes out. There was even a mural of Granny painted inside. The interior was pink, which is her favorite color. I couldn't wait to see it in person.

"This is so beautiful. I don't understand how you were able to do all of this without me not knowing."

"You had a lot on your plate, and I just wanted to pull my weight with what I could do."

"I'm so blessed to have married you. I love you so much." I got up to kiss his lips.

"I just want my woman to be set for life. You don't know how much I love you, Keyshia. I know I love you more than you love me. It's not even a competition. I need you, baby."

"I need you too, Khalil."

I was so emotional I couldn't stop the waterworks. We ate our dinner and continued with our great conversation. Once we were done, we went inside the bathroom, and he filled the tub for my bubble bath. He stayed with me, and once I laid back in the tub, he rubbed my feet. Just feeling his presence here was amazing. This is something I'd always value and could never forget. I appreciate how he has been my rock throughout this pregnancy.

Chapter 16

Erin Jackson

I felt the butterflies swarm around my stomach when my name was called to receive my certificate. I stood up cheerfully and grabbed it while I smiled for pictures. I worked my ass for the last ten months to achieve this goal. Now today, I get to celebrate all of my hard work and dedication. I turned red seeing how hard Mike and Kiki cheered for me.

The graduation was over pretty fast. I got so many hugs and flowers from everybody. I'm so ready to get out of here and celebrate. Our house was beautifully decorated and awaiting my arrival. Tomorrow morning Mike was taking me to Las Vegas for a weekend getaway. I couldn't be any more excited.

"Congratulations, sister." Keyshia hugged me tightly. "Granny would be proud of you."

"I know she would." We all left the school and headed to my house.

"I'm so fucking proud of you, babe." Mike leaned over and kissed me as he drove.

"Daddy, pay attention!" Kiki snapped.

"I got it, damn."

"I can't believe I did it man." I let out a sigh of relief.

"You earned this."

"I really did."

"You ready to have fun?" He asked.

"I wanna get filthy drunk, but I'ma behave myself. I don't want to be too hungover for our trip tomorrow." He chuckled. I plan on having a nasty ass vacation tomorrow. Plenty of rough sex, drinks, and gambling.

We pulled up to the house, and everybody was right behind us. I rushed inside because I couldn't wait any longer. I took pictures with everybody before changing into a comfortable, sexy dress. I'm ready to party and turn up now that I feel comfortable. I have wanted to let loose for a while, and now is the perfect time.

We partied until midnight, and that was only because Mike and I had to be up early to get to the airport. If not, who knows when all of our guests would have gone home. Once my house was cleaned and I showered, I climbed into the bed and looked at the pictures from my big day. I wore a proud smile in all of my photos. I never thought I could accomplish something so great, so this is a big moment for me.

"Did you enjoy yourself?" Mike asked, getting in the bed with me.

"I had a blast." I smiled.

"I'm glad you did."

"Was Kiki sad when you dropped her off home?" I felt sad Mike had to take her home early. I promised her that when we got back, we'll plan a family trip with just us three.

"You know she was, but she was talking about this trip you promised her."

"That was the only way I could get her to relax." I giggled.

"I got you something." He reached into the nightstand and pulled out two gift boxes.

"Ooh, something shiny," I said, knowing what the gifts were from the boxes.

He gifted me a diamond Cartier watch and a new chain with my name that blinded me. I loved my gifts and will wear them tomorrow on our trip. I leaned over and gave him a big kiss. I truly am loved.

"Thank you so much, babe. Not only for the gifts but for everything. I never thought I would be in so love with a man who would positively push me to want better for myself. You are a breath of fresh air in my dark world. You give me hope, and I love you so much."

"Don't keep claiming that your world is still dark. That shit is in the past. You have done so much to lighten your world. You are at peace now, and it's time to enjoy it."

"You are right." I agreed.

We talked a little more before turning off the lights and dozing off. We both felt tipsy as fuck, and as much as I wanted to fuck the shit out of him right now, we would miss our flight. The next morning, we woke up at seven o'clock. It was too fucking early, but I wasn't complaining. I know the next three days will be filled with fun. We both needed this little getaway.

The first thing I did was take care of my hygiene. We had to leave in under an hour to make it on time to board our flight. The airport was always packed at this time of the morning, and we had to stop and get breakfast. Our luggage was already packed, thank God. After I was done with my skincare regiment, I got myself dressed. I had been tracking the weather in Las Vegas on my phone, and it is hot as fuck. This whole weekend I planned to wear my hoochie mama attire.

"Good morning, babe." I pecked Mike as he got up to go to the bathroom.

"Morning, babe."

I finished getting myself together and putting on my new gifted jewelry from Mike. I opened my suitcase one last time to make sure I wasn't missing anything. I did the same to Mike's suitcase too. Once everything was checked and good to go, I waited around for Mike to be ready. He didn't take a long time. He grabbed our suitcases, and we left. I decided to eat breakfast at the airport. I'll find something once I get to my terminal. I didn't want to risk getting stuck in traffic.

We made it to the airport in an hour. It took so long because we had to find parking. Once we were inside, we checked in and went to find breakfast. I felt butterflies in my stomach all over again. I don't know why I felt nervous. It's not like Mike and I haven't had a vacation before. I guess it's just my mushy ass feeling all in love again, and I can't wait to spend alone time with my man.

It didn't take us long to board our flight. It was only forty-five minutes long, which is exactly what I needed. We talked the entire time, so we both could stay awake. My hangover was kicking my ass this morning.

I was thrilled when the plane landed. We went to get our luggage and check-in for our rental car. The closer we got to checking into our hotel, the more nervous I became. I was so excited, and I couldn't contain myself. I felt like a kid in a candy store. Mike picked up the rental, and we drove to our hotel. We stayed at the Waldorf Astoria. We received our room keys and headed up to our floor. I gasped when I opened the door, and there were congratulation balloons and rose petals all over the room. I couldn't believe he set this up for me.

"Aww, thank you, babe." I hugged him tightly.

"It's a lot more surprises coming." He spent a bag on my celebration already. I couldn't imagine what the next surprise would be.

"Oh really?" I smirked.

"Get dressed. We are going to brunch."

I did as he said because I didn't want to ruin any surprises. I freshened up, and so did he. We left and headed to the strip, where he had a full day planned for us. We went to brunch and had an amazing time like I knew we would.

Chapter 17

Khalil "Bully" Wright

I woke up to Keyshia yelling my name at the top of her lungs. I jumped up, worrying that something was wrong. She lay across the bed in a puddle of water. Her water broke. This is the moment. I'm really about to be a dad.

"What do you need me to do?" I helped her sit up.

"Help me take a shower. We gotta get to the hospital." She didn't look to be in pain, just nervous.

I carefully lifted her and helped her into the shower. I scrubbed her body and helped rinse her off. She told me which dress she wanted out of her closet so she could easily slip into it. Once she was dressed, I got myself together. Her nerves seemed to calm down, and she wasn't in a rush.

"Why you not hurrying up?" I asked her.

"I don't have any contractions yet. My water broke for sure, though." She drank a glass of water.

"What do you want me to do?" I asked again because we were on a time limit before KJ started to push his head through.

"Just let's wait a moment. Let me call Erin and tell her the news."

She pulled her phone out of her purse and called Erin on speaker. She answered right away.

"Hello?" She answered.

"My water broke," Keyshia said.

"Bitch, why are you so calm?" It sounded like she woke them up. I could hear Mike in the background. It was four in the morning.

"I don't have any contractions yet."

"Well, before you get to the hospital, you should get something to eat because they won't allow you to eat until you give birth. Hopefully, KJ doesn't take too long."

"You're right. We'll stop at McDonald's for breakfast."

"How's Bully?"

"He's right here looking at me like I'm a serial killer because I'm so calm."

"I'm at home looking at you like you're a serial killer. I don't know why the fuck you're so calm and not panicking. You are about to push a baby through your vagina."

"It's no reason to panic until the pain comes. Our hospital bags are at the door waiting, the car seat is already installed, and his nursery is completed. I'm just anxiously waiting to meet my baby boy."

"Well, I guess it doesn't sound as bad when you say it like that."

"Alright, I'll call you once we get checked into the hospital."

"I'll be there as soon as they let visitors in."

"Alright, I love you."

"I'm praying for a safe delivery. I can't wait to meet you auntie's baby boy. I love you guys!"

"We love you too."

She hung up with a smile on her face. She looked peaceful. I thought today would be a rollercoaster of emotions for her since Granny wasn't here to experience the birth. My woman is strong, and she's holding it together. On the other hand, I thought I would be out of it and have flashbacks of April and our daughter Olivia. For some reason, I'm not feeling what I thought I would have. It's all about Keyshia and KJ, and I'm not scared like I thought I would have been. I can't wait to have my child in my hands soon finally.

"I love you, baby." I kissed her lips.

"I love you more. We'll be a family of three in a couple of hours." I smiled because I loved the sound of it.

"Just let me know when you are ready to go."

"Hold on. We gotta pack a couple of snacks before we go. If they say no, I can't eat. You sneak me a little bit of a KitKat." She giggled.

"I got you, mama." I chuckled. "I'ma keep this one in my pocket just for you." I slid the KitKat into my joggers.

"See, that's why I'm so in love with you. You just understand me."

I packed a few things in our pantry before we left. I helped her into the car and then loaded the bags into the backseat before driving to get her breakfast. We pulled into the McDonald's thrive-thru and ordered. I don't know how she had an appetite right now, but she sure did eat.

"That was good." She smiled.

"It better have been good. You spent thirty-six dollars at cheap ass McDonald's."

"Let's just go."

I started up the car and drove to the hospital after

we finished breakfast. I got more excited the closer we got, but that's when she started to feel her contractions coming. It started small but worsened as we checked into labor and delivery. She had to be seated in a wheelchair to take her into her room.

"It fucking hurts!" She grunted as I helped her change out of her dress into the gown they provided.

I didn't know what to tell her, so I just helped as much as possible. She wore the pain on her face while the nurses poked her arms with needles to give her an IV. I stayed by her bedside, observing her. Sadly there was nothing I could do to help her at this moment. She's strong through. I texted Erin and let her know we were here already. She asked how Keyshia looked, and I said in pain because I didn't know what she meant. She called me on FaceTime.

"Let me see her."

I turned the camera around.

"I'm getting up now, Keysh. I'll be there very soon. I'll do your hair and get you all dolled up." Keyshia smiled, and that's all I wanted.

The nurse checked her cervix and said she was six centimeters dilated and needed to get to ten before she could start pushing. Some guy came in right after and placed an epidural in her back. She was crying on the pillow the nurse gave her to hug so she could be still. I felt so sorry for her. The pain was atrocious. It took about five minutes or a little less for her to feel better after the epidural.

"I can't feel my legs." She half smiled.

"You thuggin' this shit out, bae."

"All this time, I was excited to have a baby, but I don't know if I ever thought about how is he supposed to slide out of my pussy." She shrugged.

I chuckled. The medicine was getting to her.

"Are you still anxious?" I asked.

"I just want to get it over with. This shit fucking hurts." She frowned.

"It'll be over soon, babe."

It was now just turning six in the morning. A nurse came into the room to ask if Erin was allowed to come into the room. Keyshia gave her permission, and soon Erin came with flowers, balloons, and a teddy bear for KJ.

"Oh my God, this is really happening." She kissed Keyshia's belly before coming to hug me.

"Look at you looking slow. You about to be a daddy. Perk up. Turn on some music in here." She punched my arm.

"I'm tired as hell. We just went to sleep when her water broke."

"Damn. I'ma leave you alone then." She giggled. "Mike said he'll be here later. You told him to handle something, so he's working on it." She shrugged.

I nodded. I sat on the uncomfortable couch and watched Erin fix Keyshia's hair with a flat iron. I'm sure she wasn't supposed to plug into the outlet. She then did her makeup. My girl did look good, though. Erin took many pictures of Keyshia in the bed then I jumped in a lot of the pictures too. I was excited.

"Sorry, dear, I have to recheck your cervix." The nurse came in.

We moved out of her way, and she said Keyshia was now nine centimeters dilated. We all looked at each other with wide eyes. I don't know how long it will take to reach ten centimeters, but it'll be very soon.

We tried to keep her in good spirits and make her

laugh. I didn't want her to think of the pain or Granny's absence. So far, she has been doing a great job. It took an hour for the next cervix check. She was fully dilated, and my heart dropped.

"Dad, grab this leg, and we'll place it here." I followed the nurse and did as she said.

Her legs were wide open, and she gripped the bed rails. Her eyes looked scared. I bent over and kissed her lips before rubbing her head.

"You are the strongest person I know. You got this shit, ma." She smiled.

"Just the three of us." She said in a whisper before the nurse told her to start pushing.

"One, two, three, push."

"One, two, three, push."

"Ahhh!"

"One, two, three, push."

"Ahhh!"

"Come on. You got it." The nurse tried to cheer her on.

"I give up. I'm done." I can't believe she stopped in the middle of her pushing. She had an attitude and wasn't budging.

"No, you can't give up. You for real got this, babe. Come on, hold my hand. Erin grab her other hand." I had to speak up 'cause what the fuck did she mean she's done?

While she pushed, I talked her through it. I told her much I love her and how strong she is. By now, we could see his head poking through, and the nurse called for the doctor to come in and finish. She came in just a couple of minutes later.

"He has a head full of hair," I said, peaking at his head. I couldn't believe this was real. Erin set up her camera to record a video while she snapped photos with my phone.

"I feel like I'm pushing out a bowling ball." Her face was upset.

"Great job, mama. I want you to do the same thing. One, two, three, push and hold it. Your baby boy is almost out." The doctor positioned herself for Keyshia to push.

She started to push, and I saw KJ slowly coming out. My eyes couldn't stop watering. I thought I would've been murdered by now or would have killed myself after April passed away. I never imagined living life again to this full extent. Keyshia came into my life and saved me.

"Push, push, push, push!" The doctor and the nurses yelled.

The doctor pulled out KJ and laid him on Keyshia's chest. She busted out in tears, and Erin captured it all on video.

"Oh my God. My baby boy." She cried with KJ.

The nurse took him over to a table to clean him up. While I cut off the remainder of his umbilical cord while they cared for KJ, I walked back and forth, ensuring Keyshia was okay while the doctor pushed out her placenta.

Everything was moving so quickly. I had an out-of-body experience witnessing this. KJ's cries made my heart beat. It didn't take long before the doctor was done with Keyshia. She was cleaned up, and they fixed her bed for her to sit up.

"Here you go, mama." The nurse opened the front of her gown and placed KJ in her arms. She cried and kissed him immediately.

"You look just like your daddy." She silently cried.

"Here, babe." She handed me KJ. I sat on the edge of

the bed next to her.

Immediately my heart felt warm. He did look just like me. My seed. My everything. A new beginning. I kissed Keyshia, and we both couldn't stop smiling.

"He is so handsome. You did a great job Keysh." Erin said, standing next to us.

"I didn't think I could do it anymore. I'm just glad he's here and healthy."

We just all stared at him silently. Our lives changed forever. I know Keyshia feels the same way I feel. I'm just in shock that he's finally here.

"Damn, I didn't call my mama," I said, remembering.

"Mike handled it. She said to let her know when she is welcome to come. She wanted to give you guys your space."

"Call her babe," Keyshia said.

I called her on FaceTime. She answered immediately and cried when her eyes fell on KJ.

"Where you at? Come on, lady. Your grandson wants to meet you." Keyshia excitedly yelled into the phone.

"Oh my God. I'll be there in fifteen minutes. I was out looking for a gift to bring."

"You don't need to bring a gift. Just come." I told her.

"I'm on my way."

One of the nurses returned with ice chips for Keyshia and showed her how to breastfeed. KJ latched on to her nipple and ate. Keyshia said it felt weird, but she was excited. For the next hour, we celebrated with our closest friends and family. I was waiting for Mike to get here because he had to pick up Keyshia's push present.

She told me over and over that women get gifts for giving birth. I already knew what to get her and couldn't wait to see her facial expression when I gave it to her. Mike called when he was downstairs checking in. I went down there to meet him. I was excited as fuck.

"Nigga looking like he's walking on the moon right now." He smiled when I approached.

"I am." I chuckled.

"Congratulations. Come on, let me see my nephew."

"Let me make sure it's the correct gift."

"Nah, the lady wrapped it good. I took a video of her doing it. I forgot to send it to you."

He showed me the video, which was the right gift I ordered. We went upstairs to go back into the room. We both washed our hands when we entered the room.

"Hi, mama." He greeted my mom, who was the closest.

"Congratulations, sister." He walked over to Keyshia, hugging her.

"Welcome to the world, nephew." He gazed at KJ.

"Here you go." She handed him KJ to hold.

"Damn, you really a dad." He said to me.

"Anyways, I love you, and thank you for having my son." I held up the orange Hermes gift bag. Her mouth dropped, and excitement filled her eyes.

"No, you didn't!" She almost jumped out of bed.

I handed her the gift bag. She ripped through it to get to the beige Birkin bag. She cried again, which she had been doing all day.

"Thank you so much, baby."

"You deserve it, especially after witnessing all the pain you just went through."

"You're so sweet." She couldn't take her eyes off her

bag.

Logic went to get us food, and we all just hung out. Every time KJ cried, everybody jumped up to see what was wrong. It felt good to have a big support system. I went with him when KJ had to leave for his newborn testing. I wasn't letting him leave my eyesight.

Chapter 18

Keyshia Wright

Postpartum is kicking my ass. KJ is a week old now. My body feels so different, and it's taking me some time to adjust. My pussy was so swollen the first few days after birth. I was hardly able to sit down comfortably without crying. I had one tear that needed sutures.

On top of that, breastfeeding after labor fucking hurts. It felt like I was having contractions all over again. I wasn't prepared for that at all. I felt guilty switching him to formula instead of my breast milk, but I couldn't do it any longer for the sake of my body and mind. Everybody understood and supported my decision. That day Erin helped by going to Target and picking up the formula and bottles I'd need to transition KJ. It took a little time for him to accept the bottle, but when he did, it helped ease a lot of pressure.

My body is healing. I was in no rush to look like myself before I got pregnant. I'm taking this all in with honor. I can't believe I'm somebody's mama. I find myself sleeping less so that I can stare at my baby. He's so perfect to me. I catch him smiling at times, and my heart swells. I'm so in love with the baby we made.

Bully has been an amazing help to me. He gets up in the middle of the night for KJ's feedings and does whatever I'm not physically able to do. I'm finally back on my feet and moving with minimal pain. Today I set up an at home newborn photoshoot. I wanted to capture this moment forever. Our whole family is here to witness KJ taking these pictures. I'm so glad I have them in my life.

"Oh my gosh, look at my grandson." Bully's mom said, looking at KJ lying on his stomach while the photographer snapped photos of him sleeping.

I agreed with her. KJ is so freaking adorable. He looked identical to Bully's baby pictures. He had no features of mine, but hopefully, that changes as he grows. After the photographer left, Erin and Bully's mom cleaned up, so I didn't have to bend.

"Keyshia, I cannot wait to see those photos." Bully's mom said while I fed KJ.

"I know I cannot wait either! She said she'll email them to me in two days, and I'm so anxious."

"Back in the day, we couldn't take these extravagant photoshoots. I haven't seen any pictures as cute as his setup."

"You give me baby fever." Erin sat down on the couch.

"So I'm getting a niece or a nephew?" I asked.

"I said baby fever. I'm not going to dive into parenthood." She laughed.

"Girl, goodbye." I waved her off.

Bully, and Mike came into the living room. He was dressed from head to toe, so I knew he was leaving. It sucked that he had business to handle. He came home early every night to help with KJ, but he was gone for most of the day. I always had either Bully's mom or Erin here to help with anything I needed, but I still wished it was him here.

"I'll be back, babe." He bent down to kiss me.

I wanted to show him my puppy dog eyes, but I left it alone. If he said he had stuff to do, I know he's telling the truth. He wouldn't be in the streets knowing he has a baby that's only days old. He's not the kind of guy to waste time anyways. I watched as he and Mike left without a care in the world.

"Why do you look so sad?" Erin asked me.

"I didn't want him to leave," I admitted.

"Why you didn't tell him that?" She asked.

"He has work to do at the club. I didn't want him prolonging anything."

"You're so understanding 'cause my ears are disconnected when it comes to my hearing. You're leaving to go where?" She joked, acting as if she couldn't hear.

"I try not to be crazy. You know I could go there, but it's no reason to be." I shrugged it off.

"Well, do you have anything you want to eat today?" She asked.

"Chinese food would be amazing."

"I'll go pick that up." She smiled.

Erin has been here every day until Bully comes home. She has turned into my personal caregiver while I recovered. She was right there when I couldn't move fast enough to get KJ out of his bassinet. I don't know how to thank her for washing our clothes, cleaning the house, and prepping meals for me. She is a blessing because I could hardly do anything while I adjusted to motherhood.

"Seriously, I can't wait for you to have a baby. I'ma

be there just like you're here for me right now."

"You know I got you. That's what family do. Shit, you're the only one I have." She shook her head.

"Well, you are all I have left too." I laughed because it was true.

My phone buzzed with a text message. I smiled, seeing Jasmine checking on me. She asked to come over to meet KJ in person. She has received tons of pictures but wanted to give me space until I was ready to welcome visitors. I gave her the green light to come over.

While Erin left to pick up lunch, Bully's mom was in the kitchen cleaning out the refrigerator. KJ was in my arms, falling asleep from the bottle I had just given him. Looking into his eyes, I felt sad, thinking of my Granny, but I kept my composure. I was tired of crying, honestly. I just wanted to celebrate her life instead of feeling the emptiness.

"Granny would have spoiled you rotten." I kissed his little nose before placing him in the bassinet beside the couch.

I went into the kitchen to help Bully's mom. I loved this woman so much, and I thank her for stepping in and treating me like one of her own. She has respected me and has given me so much love it's hard to tell if she's my biological mom or Bully's. Don't let the niceness fool you because she tears my ass up when she's mad. She doesn't play. She tells me when I'm wrong and agrees with me when I'm right.

"If you don't take your ass back on that couch. You are supposed to be sitting down relaxing or taking a nap while he sleeps." She reprimanded me.

"I'm not tired, though. I just want somebody to talk to me." I pouted.

"Hi, daughter-in-law. How are you doing today?" She switched up the conversation laughing.

"I am bored out of my mind! Thanks to you and Erin, everything in the house is always clean, so I have nothing to do."

"You are welcome." Sarcastically she smiled. I left her alone because she was crazy sometimes. The doorbell rang, and I got up to answer it before she beat me to the punch.

"Heyyy." Jasmine walked through the door with gifts.

"How are you? Come in." We hugged before she entered.

"Let me wash my hands. I cannot wait to see his cute self." She went into the kitchen and greeted Lori before washing her hands.

We all went into the living room, where KJ was asleep. She was so excited to see him for the first time. I opened the gifts she brought and was so happy that I had great friends. She bought KJ tons of clothes and teddy bears. Now that our children are cousins, it was our job to keep them together.

"He is so handsome, Keysh. He looks just like his daddy, but when he sleeps, he looks just like you." She looked over at him while he slept.

"I say the same thing too. He took his newborn pictures today."

"I need a picture when you get them." I showed her the pictures on my phone that we took. I know it is not the professional one, but I couldn't resist capturing so many photos of him.

Erin had come back with our lunch. She made everybody a plate of the delicious Chinese food. When KJ woke up, Jasmine took over because she wanted to hold him really bad. We all kicked it until she had to leave and pick up her babies from school.

Chapter 19

Erin Jackson

I haven't been to work in three and a half weeks. Bully was okay with it and still paid me. I have been with Keyshia every day, helping her regain her strength and catch up with some much needed sleep. I'm so happy my nephew is here. He is a handsome little baby. Tonight I needed to come to work. I couldn't be gone too long. It was 6 pm, and I texted Bully, letting him know I came in tonight, so he has a set of eyes here. He has been popping in here and there since KJ was born. Nobody has gotten back to the full swing of things yet.

The club doors weren't opened for customers yet. All the staff was here preparing for their arrival. I did my rounds, ensuring my girls had everything needed to provide the best experience for all the VIP customers. It took me an hour and a half. As I walked to the bar to check something, I saw Pamela sitting there scrolling on her phone. I ignored her because I couldn't stand that bitch either. She's a kiss ass whenever Bully is around. She wants him to notice her so badly, and her dumb ass can't see that he won't.

As I walked past, I saw her stalking Keyshia's Instagram because she was looking at the photo of KJ she had just posted today. My blood instantly boiled. Keyshia made it known she didn't fuck with her from the beginning, so what was the point of stalking her page? You already wanna fuck her husband. She deserves her ass beaten, and I'll gladly do it.

"They are a happy family, and you seem bothered by it." I walked up behind her.

"What are you talking about?" She locked her phone quickly.

"Bully would beat your ass himself for fucking with his woman and child." I made that shit clear because it's true.

"You don't even know what you're talking about it." She tried to get up and walk off.

"I do." I pulled out my phone and showed her the video I recorded of her being nosey. It was a clear video of her scrolling through Keyshia's Instagram page and checking her comments. Her mouth dropped.

"Check this out. I am very overprotective of my sister and my nephew. I'll give you the option to catch this fade right here or outside." She tried to move out of the way, but I pulled her back and sent punches to her body and face. I was still cautious not to break anything because I didn't want Bully to be mad about the fight. She swung a couple of times but never connected to anything. I grabbed her by the back of her head and smushed her face into the bar.

"Stop fucking with my motherfucking family. Bully will deal with you later." I slammed her face one last time before walking away.

I was so fucking pissed I had to get out of character. Bully and Keyshia didn't need that kind of drama because they were still exhausted from having a newborn on their hands. I went upstairs and called Keyshia. Hopefully, I wasn't waking her up from a nap.

"Hey, boo." She answered cheerfully.

"Where is Bully?" I asked.

"Downstairs. Why? Did something happen?"

"Put me on speaker phone and go get him," I instructed.

She yelled for him to come upstairs. I heard him enter the room.

"What happened, Erin?" He asked.

"I'm making sure everything is taken care of before opening. I'm walking to the bar to make sure my girls have what they need, and Pamela is sitting there on her phone. I walk up behind her and see KJ's pictures on her screen. I stand there and wait while she's scrolling and looking through Keyshia's Instagram pictures. Hold on; I took a video for proof. I'm sending it to you right now. I confront her, and she tells me I didn't see anything. I show her that I recorded her and told her to come catch this fade."

"Wait, y'all fought?" Keyshia sounded shocked.

"Mopped her ass all up and down the bar." I proudly said.

Keyshia was dying laughing. "Where the fuck she at now?" Bully was pissed.

"She better be down there working. I'm not sure, though. I came upstairs to call you guys."

"I'm on my way." He handed the phone back to Keyshia.

"I hope he's not mad," I said to her.

"Girl, you know he doesn't give a fuck. He's been telling her ass that she's been on thin ice. I had already seen this problem coming from the day we interviewed her. Her previous work experience is impeccable, but she's unprofessional. This man has told you a million times to stay out of his way and do your job; she still can't do that."

"That bitch is obsessed."

"She is so damn slow. She's about to lose a great paying job over nothing. At least if I'ma risk, my job, I better have gotten a taste of the dick." She laughed. This bitch is crazy too 'cause I don't know why she thinks it funny.

"Girl, goodbye, go take care of your baby." I hung up the phone.

I went back downstairs since the doors were about to open. I then went into the locker room to check on my girls. Their outfits were on point, and the best thing is they listened to whatever I said. I haven't had any problems with them yet. They come to work and get the job done. Bully was here in less than an hour. When he walked through the door, he was pissed. He told me to go to his office while he looked for Pamela. I did as he said and waited at his door. It was locked. He came ten minutes later with Pamela trailing behind him. He unlocked his door and sat on the couch while she stood by the door like a child.

"What the fuck happened?" He asked Pamela. She stood there speechless. "Speak." He didn't stutter.

"She attacked me."

"Tell him the real reason why I attacked you. Tell the story right, or I'll show the video in 4K of you being a thirsty ass hoe." I smiled.

She looked at Bully with tears in her eyes. "I already know what happened." He got up from behind his desk and walked up to her by grabbing her throat and hemming her up against the wall. "Bitch I have warned you every day since I met your bird ass to respect my wife and stay the fuck out of my way. I don't want your trifling ass. Nothing about you I would even touch bitch. Get your shit and get the fuck out of my club!"

Damn, I felt the anger in his voice. He let her throat go, and she gasped for air before scurrying out of his office. He went back to sit down, but he looked like he was trying to calm his nerves. I felt terrible for him. He was trying to run a business but has had a rollercoaster of emotions ever since this club opened. I got up to leave and gave him some space.

"Can you take over for the weekend, and I'll give you next weekend off and double the pay? I gotta get someone in here ASAP to fill her position."

"You good, bro. I'll do whatever to help out. Just let me know what you need. Probably look into that guy that you said was the second best. I'm sure he'll be a better fit."

"Thanks, sis."

I nodded before walking out of his office and going downstairs into the club. By now, the crowd had made its way in, and it was packed. There were plenty of people in the VIP section, and the first person I spotted was my sexy ass man. I walked over to make sure he had everything he needed.

"Damn." He said when I approached.

"Damn is right." I spun around for him to see my dress.

"Wassup, babe." He stood up to kiss me.

"You won't believe what happened tonight."

"What?" He looked curious to know.

"I fought Pamela."

"Bully knows?"

"Yes. He's in the office. He just got here and fired her."

"I'ma go upstairs and will be back." He got up and left.

One of my girls brought over bottles to his table. He was there with a bunch of niggas as always. I went to do my rounds and keep myself busy. Now I had an entire weekend to cover. It's okay because family takes care of each other.

Bully and Mike walked up to me an hour later. Bully handed me a set of keys to his office if I needed to make myself comfortable during my new weekend shift. That was out of love because Pamela didn't have his office keys. He thanked me and headed home. Mike said he would stay with me the whole weekend since he wanted to make sure I could handle it on my own. I was cool with that. I wanted my man around regardless, so this was just a plus.

When I got tired, I went into the office to lay on the couch. My feet were killing me. When I was a bottle girl, I didn't wear heels to work. With my position now, I wear heels every night and never take them off. Mike came upstairs with me. I put my order in with the kitchen, so I could eat something while I relaxed.

"So, did Bully tell you what happened?" I asked Mike while he rubbed my feet.

"He said a little something." He chuckled.

"I fucked her up."

"Okay, Muhammad Ali." We both fell out laughing.

"Anyways, how is the barbershop coming along? I didn't get the chance to ask you earlier."

"It's taking longer than expected since we had to rebuild everything from the ground up."

"I'm glad you got all new everything. It was looking

like you were stuck in the eighties." I giggled.

"That's exactly what it looked like."

"I'm proud of you, though."

"Thanks, babe."

"Something is on your mind. I can tell. What is it?"

I know my man like the back of his hand. He was tiptoeing around something. He just didn't know how to tell me, and it made me nervous. I pray it's nothing bad.

"Damn, get out of my face." He chuckled.

"I'm serious. What's wrong, babe? You okay?" I asked.

"I'm good."

"Whatever. Since we lie to each other now."

"Nobody is lying to you. You just ruin everything."

"Ruin what?" I asked, confused.

"Close your eyes, and don't look." He sounded pissed.

I looked at him strangely but closed my eyes. I felt him move my legs off his lap, and he stood up. "Open your eyes."

My mouth dropped. He was on one knee, holding out a diamond engagement ring.

"I love you, Erin. I'm in love with you. I wanna be your husband and give you everything your heart desires. You are a good woman. You're loyal as fuck. You stepped in as a stepmom to my daughter, and I didn't even ask you to do that. You mean everything to Kiki and me. We just want to make you a part of our family officially. Will you marry me?"

"Yes, yes, yes, yes," I yelled and cried. "I love you so much." We kissed, slipping our tongues in and out of each other's mouths. I couldn't believe it.

"I'm crazy over you, girl."

"I'm crazy over you too." I smiled.

Now that was a great secret he was keeping from me. I would never have expected this. There were no signs he was going to propose. We talked about marriage, of course, but I didn't know he had a ring in his pocket.

"Did I ruin your surprise?" I asked.

"You sure did, but it's okay. I picked up the ring this afternoon, and it's been burning a hole in my pocket. I had something set up for you, but we can still do it. You just received the proposal earlier than expected. I can't hide shit from you."

"Well, that's good. Don't hide anything from me." I giggled.

I forgot I ordered food for us to eat during my break. I didn't care anymore; I was just stunned. I took a picture of my hand and sent it to Keyshia. I thought she would be asleep, but she was up and replied immediately.

Bestie: Oh my fucking gosh! Congratulations! That's a pretty ass ring.

Mike helped me put back on my heels so I could get back to work. I had three more hours until the club closed. I couldn't wait to get home and make love to my man. I needed to show him how grateful I was for this surprise proposal.

Chapter 20

Pamela Davis

I don't know how I got caught up in my cousin's web of tricks. My life was going great, and one wrong decision to apply for a job my cousin referred me to turned my life upside down. Tori was so in love with Bully, and I see why. That man is so captivating. I have never even touched him, but I sadly fell in love with him too. I looked forward to seeing him at the club. He wasn't constantly snapping at me, but he also wasn't joking with me either.

Don't get me wrong; I applied for the job because I needed it. Since Tori was the one that told me about it, she wanted me to spy and see what information I could get about Keyshia and Bully. Tori hated her. She said ever since Bully met her; her life spiraled downhill. She had always bragged about this boss ass nigga she was with, but nobody ever saw him but her. She then explained their relationship and how he completely ghosted her. That was some fucked up shit. On top of that, Keyshia has a nasty ass attitude. Every time I saw her, she had her nose twisted up like she was a goddess or something.

"So you really not gonna tell me what happened last night?" Tori asked while she made herself a cup of coffee.

She had moved in with me after she was evicted from her apartment. Bully kept up with her rent and bills until Keyshia came along. She was down bad, and my ass is down too. I don't know how she hasn't been able to secure a job in the two years they haven't been together. I guess she was working overtime to try and get him back. I could see her waiting for me to answer her question. I don't know how to tell her I fell for the same man she is in love with.

"I fought her friend that works at the club. After I whooped her ass, he came and fired me. I'm sure Keyshia had something to do with it." I lied. My head is still ringing from our fight. Erin slammed my head into the bar hard. I should press charges against her ass.

"Pam, your face was bruised when you came home last night. You didn't look like you won."

"You look like you're staying here with me for free and will soon not have a place for you to sleep." She stopped while she was ahead.

"I can't believe this. This bitch blew up my life." She paced back and forth. She picked up her phone and dialed his number, but it went straight to voicemail. He still had her blocked.

"Fuck!" She shouted.

"What are you going to do?" I asked because I really wanted to know.

"I'ma just have to go to the club and hope I see him."

"Well, wait a week or two. I told you he wasn't coming in like that because he was with his baby."

"Fuck that ugly ass baby. Probably ain't even his anyways."

I nodded in agreement with her because she

wanted to believe that. His baby looked exactly like him, and there was no denying that. I didn't want to hear any more about it, so I got up to leave. Now that I'm out of a job, I have a lot of expenses to cut out. I had a little savings, but it would only last for two months. I really needed to get my job back. I could already tell Bully wouldn't give me a second chance. I'll try, though.

I walked into the parking garage and got into my car. The first thing I did was call Bully to see if he would accept my apology. I cried all the way home last night. I had never seen him so angry, and he definitely was mad at me. The businesswoman in me wanted to threaten him with a lawsuit for putting his hands on me, but I knew well enough that man would kill me and show up to my funeral. The phone rang, but I didn't get an answer. At least he didn't block me like he did Tori. That made me feel a little good inside.

I drove off and headed to the gym. I needed a clear mind to figure out what I would do. I didn't want to get evicted like Tori. I can't see myself staying with my mom. I just need to put my hustle shoes on and grind it out. After I receive my last check, I only have a little time to make something happen.

Chapter 21

Michael "Mike" Simmons

I had a live DJ spinning all of the latest hits and an open bar for the grand opening of my barbershop Grand Kutz. This place was remodeled from top to bottom to pass the state board's inspection. Plus, a business on Melrose Ave is a lot of competition. There are so many barbershops, clothing stores, and shoe reselling stores. You have to step your game up down here.

I have been open for an hour, and it has been packed ever since. I had a lineup of fifteen barbers making Grand Kutz one of the biggest barbershops on Melrose. There's an upstairs and downstairs to hold everybody. Uncle Ronnie was walking around, taking it all in and greeting customers.

"This is some amazing shit, nephew." He said, dapping me up.

"I appreciate it. It's time to collect this money."

"For sure." He said before walking off.

"I was looking for you." Erin walked up to me with a glass of champagne in her hand.

"You good, babe?"

"I'm doing amazing. I just can't stop saying how amazing this place looks." She complimented.

"The hard work is paying off."

While we talked, some light skin nigga approached her. I was about to escort him the fuck out, but he started to say some wild shit that made me and her look at each other crazy.

"I saw you on the Grand Kutz Instagram page a month ago when the owner posted you cleaning up. I know for a fact you are my sister. My mom is Brenda Rodriguez-Jackson, and I believe you are my sister."

Suddenly Erin's face turned red, and she looked ill immediately. "Back up from my girl, my nigga." I pushed him away.

"She was pregnant with me when our father was sent to jail. I just want to talk to you and ask a few questions."

"Leave me alone, go away! What the fuck is wrong with you people?" She screamed and stormed off. By now, everyone downstairs had turned their attention to us to see what was happening.

"Get the fuck up outta here."

I grabbed him by the shirt and dragged his ass out. I prayed Erin was okay because he doesn't know what trauma he just opened up. Bully looked at me crazy, and he came with me to find Erin. She was in the break room crying with Keyshia.

"You good, babe?" I rubbed her back.

"Did he leave?" She asked.

"I threw his ass out."

"He said my mom's full name. He looks just like my dad Mike. That nigga is really my brother." She sobbed.

"So she gave you up but kept him?" Keyshia shook her head.

"Look, I just want to fix my makeup and never

speak of this again. That shit is something I never expected. I'm doing amazing right now and don't need to backtrack. So please respect my wishes and let this be the last time we talk about the dead."

She got up and went into the restroom. No one went to follow her. This was some fucked up shit, but I'll always be in her corner when she wants to speak about it. I watched her come out of the restroom with a bright smile on her face as if nothing had happened. It's scary to see her bury her pain so deep. I allowed her to deal with her trauma on her own. If she didn't handle it correctly, we'd be back at Doctor Shonda's office for an appointment. Therapy has gotten her so far and into a great mental place. I'd hate to see her lose her cool. We all returned to the party, but we carefully watched her mannerisms.

"You think she's good?" I asked Keyshia as we stood at the bar and watched her.

"No, she's in shock and doesn't know how to express it. She'll break down soon, but it'll be when nobody is watching. I've watched her do it for years. For some reason, I have faith in her, though. Therapy has helped her, so I hope she uses her learned tools to cope with this."

"This is some crazy shit." I couldn't imagine going through what she had to experience as a child.

"I'm sure Granny is turning in her grave right now. She was so overprotective of her. She disliked her biological mom and her foster mom so much."

"I think I need to handle this one for her."

"See what she wants to do first. You never know if she may want to speak to him in the future. It may close old wounds or open new ones. You never know, but we'll be her emotional support team."

She was right. I watched as she greeted all the guests coming in and out. One thing I know about my girl is she'll dive straight into work to keep herself busy when something is on her mind. Keyshia left to find somewhere to change KJ's diaper while I went to assist Erin with a customer. I answered a few questions the customer had before they walked off. I grabbed her by the waist and hugged her tightly.

"I love you, gorgeous." She smiled.

"I love you more, handsome."

"You know I got your back and your front, right?" I asked, and she giggled.

"I know that for a fact. Nobody has ever loved me like you."

"That's all I needed to hear." I kissed her neck. "You ready to get out of here?" I asked.

"Yes, we have to make it to the realtor's office before she closes." She looked at the time on her Cartier watch.

"It's finally time to close on our house." I smiled.

It's been a long two months searching for a home, but we finally found where we wanted to live. I'm just excited we finally got our shit together. In a month, we will be celebrating our second anniversary.

"Go handle your business so we can get out of here."

"Alright."

I kissed her before finding my uncle and letting him know I was leaving. He would close up and handle the rest of the grand opening. I walked downstairs to find Erin standing in the front with Bully and Keyshia.

"Congrats on closing again," Keyshia said when I walked up.

"A big accomplishment for us." I smiled.

"Are we still meeting for dinner later?" Keyshia asked.

"Yes, 7 pm at Eddie V's." She smiled back.

"Alright, see you guys tonight."

We all walked out and went our separate ways. I helped Erin get into the car and headed to Encino to meet with the realtor. It was an hour away in traffic. As we got closer, she started to get excited. This is a big step in the right direction for us. I couldn't wait to start filling the house with our babies.

"When you gonna give me a baby?" I asked her as we pulled up.

"Soon." That was all she said. I could hear the emptiness in her voice. I hope her brother showing up didn't push her back into the dark place she was in.

I just wanted her to focus on decorating our home. She seemed excited, so that's where I wanted her to keep her focus. I made it to the office an hour before closing. We walked inside and signed our final paperwork before getting our keys and taking pictures.

Erin wanted to drive by the new house to see it before we ended our day. I followed her orders and went to our beach house in Manhattan Beach. From our home, we were able to see the beach that was two blocks away. It was a five-bedroom four car garage. I couldn't wait to move in.

We made it to the new house in fifteen minutes. I parked in the garage before we got out to take pictures of the place. Erin talked about new furniture and new appliances she wanted. We spent thirty minutes here talking about our plans before we left to go home and get ready for dinner.

We had an hour and thirty minutes before we had

to leave. We both took a shower and threw on new clothes. Erin was complaining about how cold it was and wanted to be comfortable. Once we were dressed, we left and headed to dinner. In the car, Kiki called on FaceTime, and we spoke to her as I drove.

"I wish I was there," Kiki whined as we were about to hang up the phone.

"Your daddy will pick you up in two days, and we can all go out, so you don't feel left out," Erin said.

"Okay, that sounds like a plan. Bye, love you guys." She hung up the phone.

"That girl never wants to be left out of the mix," I said before exiting the truck and opening Erin's door.

"She doesn't care to hang out with us. She wants to play babysitter to KJ. She has expressed how much she wants a baby."

"Her mama is gonna give her one if we don't first." I kissed her neck. She instantly blushed.

We walked into Eddie V's, and Erin gave the host Keyshia's name. She led us to our table, where Keyshia and Bully were already sitting and waiting for us. We greeted them before Erin took KJ out of Bully's hand. She had turned softer ever since Keyshia gave birth to KJ. I know she loved him, and he opened her eyes to a lot of things. She didn't seem as scared as she used to be. I can see she'll soon be ready to have children.

"Are you ordering a cocktail?" Erin asked Keyshia.

"I'm not sure yet. I've been sober for nine months, and I don't know how hard it'll hit me."

"I understand. In that case, I'll drink for you too." Erin giggled.

"So, how is the new house? Did you take pictures?" Keyshia asked.

"It is so beautiful y'all. I'm ready to move in like right now." Erin handed over her phone with the pictures she had taken earlier.

"I'm sure you are. This is such a huge step for you guys, so congratulations. If nobody else deserves this, y'all do."

"Thank you." We said in unison.

We all ordered our food and talked amongst ourselves. Today was a great day for me. I opened my first business with many more to come and closed on our dream home. I'm still keeping an eye out on Erin, though. She looks like she's handling herself well since the situation at the grand opening. I just know she covers up her emotions well.

Chapter 22

Keyshia Wright

This shot of Patron warmed my body instantly. I hadn't had alcohol in nine months, and it went straight to my pussy. I'm enjoying my first mommy night out with my girls, but I wanted to go home and fuck my man badly. The liquor was always talking to my pussy, and I was listening. The waiter brought out the dessert so we could hurry up and leave.

"This is so good." I took a bite of my bread pudding.

Bully rented me a Sprinter so I could safely enjoy myself with the ladies. We are having dinner at Ocean Prime, then going to the club. KJ is spending the night with his grandma, and Bully is at the club working as usual. He promised to come out of the office for a little while to hang out with me. He didn't want to be all in my space while I was having my first wild night out. I for sure will sneak upstairs, though, to get some of that dick.

Erin, Jasmine, Jasmine's sister Cheyenne, Mariah, Kaylen, and Breana came out to hang with me. We all needed the break, and so far, we have been having an amazing time. I did miss KJ so bad. I wanted to kiss his cute little face, but Lori promised me he was in good hands, and I needed to focus on having fun tonight.

"How does it feel to be a new mother?" Mariah asked.

"It feels so good, girl! I miss my baby so much right now I'm kinda sad." I giggled.

"That's expected. I'm sure he misses you too, but he's having a great time with grandma." Jasmine reassured me.

"I know, right." I finished my dessert.

I waited for the rest of the ladies to finish their desserts before we headed to the Sprinter. They were tipsy, but I felt drunk as fuck already. I texted Bully, letting him know that we were on our way. I didn't want him worrying about me. When we made it to the club, we bypassed the line. Erin stopped to hug her ugly ass cousin Dino. Bully hired him as the security for the entrance. We walked into our VIP section and immediately got to dancing. I felt hyped as fuck.

I felt like a ratchet bitch standing on the couch shaking my ass. I couldn't help but laugh out of embarrassment when Bully walked into the section. I leaped right into his arms and tongued him down. He greeted all of the ladies.

"You're having fun." He said, still carrying my spoiled ass.

"I am, but I want some of you." I bit his ear while I whispered to him. I was horny and wanted him to take advantage of me.

"You drunk as fuck." He chuckled.

"I'm tipsy, but stop playing. Come bend me over." I reached for his belt buckle.

"Not right here." He popped my hand. "I'ma bring her back y'all." Bully's voice trailed off as he took me to his office upstairs.

I wasn't supposed to have sex yet. I was only four and a half weeks postpartum. I decided that my pussy was healed enough to take the dick. I no longer had any pains, so I was good to fuck. I sloppily kissed all over him as he struggled to open the door to his office. Once we were inside, and it was locked, he wasted no time helping me undress. I aggressively ripped off his clothes before he dropped me on the couch so he could kneel and eat my pussy. I gasped right away. It felt so good. The last time I had sex was the week before I gave birth to KJ, and even then, it was a struggle because I was so uncomfortable. Right now, this is everything I needed and more. A minute didn't even go by before he slurped all my nectar out of me.

"Mmm." I moaned. I was fucking his face.

I don't know who enjoyed it more, him or me. I had to stop him so we could switch. I wanted to swallow his dick. The spit was seeping out of my mouth as I guided his dick in and out of my mouth. I enjoyed his facial expressions and grunts. He grabbed me by both of my arms and pulled me up to ride his dick. I took over by turning myself over, holding on to his knee for balance, and bounced my ass on his dick. He loved when I rode his dick reverse. He said it was something about seeing my ass bounce all over him.

"Ahh, daddy." I moaned, feeling the juices ooze out.

"I miss you, babe." He grunted.

"I miss you too, daddy."

I couldn't go anymore, but that didn't stop him. He picked me up without removing his dick from inside of me. I leaned on the couch for balance while he devoured me from the back. It was loud moans and ass clapping coming from the office. He was fucking the shit out of me and enjoyed every second of it. I missed the rough sex.

I lost count of how many times I climaxed per usual. He nutted in me, and we both needed to catch our breath. After a while, I went into the bathroom to clean myself off. That was much needed for both of us.

"That's what I'm talking about!" I said, walking back into the office and watching him drink a bottle of water. He couldn't help but laugh.

"You're a hoe when you're drunk." He chuckled.

"That's right. Your hoe correct yourself." I giggled.

"That was some good shit, though." He pecked my lips before going into the bathroom.

I went into the cabinet for the cleaning supplies to wipe off the couch. This was still a place of business minus our passionate love making sessions. At first, I was embarrassed, but now I don't care. Everybody in here has done something they weren't proud of. This is my husband and our establishment, so it doesn't matter.

Bully came out of the bathroom, and we called his mom to check on KJ. She had just laid him down to sleep after one of his many feedings. We talked a bit longer before he escorted me back into my section with the girls. He had more work to take care of in the office and didn't want to intrude any longer.

"You're a nasty ass bitch." Erin laughed when Bully walked away.

"This liquor got me fucked up!" I giggled.

I went back to dancing with them. *Throat Baby* by BRS Kash played, and my ratchet ass was showing out. I can't lie; I was feeling myself, but it abruptly stopped when I looked at the bar. I tried to look closer, making sure I saw correct. I was for sure seeing correct. It was Tori sitting at the bar, looking around. I'm sure she was searching for Bully. I thought he got rid of this bitch. She and Pamela are some thirsty ass bitches.

"What's wrong?" Jasmine asked.

"Nothing." I was irritated now.

"What happened?" Erin asked, catching on to my attitude.

"That's Tori," I said, pointing to her sitting at the bar.

"What is she doing here?" She frowned.

"Looking for Bully, I'm sure."

"Who's Tori?" Kaylen asked.

"A bitch Bully was dealing with before me." I rolled my eyes.

"Oh, one of them bitches." She rolled her eyes too.

I was going to leave it alone and try to boost my spirits back up, but I couldn't let it go. I'm tired of these hoes disrespecting me and my marriage. I am his woman, and these hoes are popping out of nowhere with an attitude towards me because he doesn't wanna fuck with them. I had enough of that shit. I took my shoes off and walked to the bar. When I roughly tapped her on her back, she rolled her eyes. She didn't see me coming.

"Here we go," she said with an attitude.

"What are you doing here?" I asked.

"Enjoying myself like you should be doing."

"Don't get smart with me bitch."

"This is a public club. I don't have to leave places because you're here. You already took my man. You're not going to take my right to enjoy myself either."

"Well, guess what bitch? He was never your man. In this motherfucking club, I have the right to refuse your business, so can you leave before I escort you out kindly from management." I sarcastically smiled.

All I saw was her hand lift, and I didn't know if she wanted to fight or not, but I dragged her down and whooped her ass. I had to sweetly get her together all the other times because I was pregnant, but now I was stomping her out. She fucked with me my whole pregnancy, so she was very deserving of this. She tried to fight back, but her strength was nothing compared to mine. She talked all that shit because I was pregnant, but now she's speechless. I just didn't understand.

"What was that shit you was saying when I was pregnant? You're a delusional ass bitch! You'll never get the chance to fuck with him again, dumb ass bitch." I kicked her in the face.

Dino pulled me off of her. I was fighting his ass too. I wanted to see blood. Before I knew it, Bully was at the bar pulling me away and cussing me out. He was so fucking angry I saw it all over his face. I didn't care 'cause I was angry too, and I have the right.

"Stop yelling at me. Get that bitch out of here!" I screamed back at him.

I couldn't hear what Bully said to Dino, but he took me upstairs into the office with all the girls. I was so fucking mad Bully had the audacity.

"Boss man said for you to stay in here." Dino stood at the door, not letting me get by.

I rolled my eyes. The girls tried to calm me down, but I wasn't hearing shit.

"I'm alright," I said so they could back off.

"I'll put your purse and heels here." Erin put my stuff behind the desk.

"Sorry, guys. I saw her, and my mind went blank. I still want to get her ass." I was livid.

Bully came into the office, looking at me like he

wanted to fuck me up. We mugged each other because who the fuck is he looking at like that? What would give him the right to be mad at me and not know the whole story?

"Dino escort the ladies to the Sprinter. Make sure the driver gets them all home safely." Everybody looked at Bully and moved out of the way. We still had our eyes set on each other until everybody left the room.

"What the fuck was that?" I yelled at him.

"You got a fucking kid Keyshia! You out here fighting like a fucking hood rat!" He yelled back.

"So you're telling me you don't have a problem when somebody bothers me?"

"You come and get me! I handle shit and take care of this family. What if that dumb ass bitch had a knife to back you off of her? You got a son to live for. Why the fuck are you letting a bird make you insecure? All this shit I do to respect you and make you feel special doesn't mean shit if a nobody could convince you to get out of character like that."

"Since my feelings don't fucking matter to you, take me home." I snatched my purse and heels from behind the desk and left out of the office, slamming the door.

I just wanted to feel pretty tonight and enjoy myself. I don't know what the fuck happened that fast that made my man switch on me. It's one thing to scold me in private but to show his ass off in front of an entire club had me pissed. I slipped on my heels and walked downstairs to the back entrance, where his truck was parked. He was right behind me, and I helped myself in. I didn't need his help. He drove in silence. He had an attitude, too, and he could keep it.

When he pulled into the garage, I quickly got out of the truck before he could put it in park. I hurriedly went inside the house so I could shower. I just wanted to wash off my night and get in bed. Bully needed to take his ass in the other room because I didn't want him breathing my air right now. I texted the ladies, letting them know I made it in the house. I texted Erin separately and told her I was coming over in the morning after I picked up KJ from his grandma's house.

I wiped off my makeup and undressed to take a shower. I heard Bully making noise in the bedroom, so I took extra long to avoid going back in the room with him. Once I heard nothing, I turned off the water and wrapped the towel around my body before entering the room. He removed his pillows from the bed. That's cool with me. I wanted him gone anyway. I dried off my skin and applied body oil before finding something comfortable to wear. I got in bed and checked my phone to see what the ladies said.

Bestie: He looked pissed. Are y'all good?

Me: He's sleeping in the guest bedroom.

Bestie: Come on, you guys. This is something small to work out. You guys shouldn't let this interfere with the peace in your marriage.

Me: He started this shit when he came downstairs and cursed me out.

Bestie: Sleep on it and have a better attitude tomorrow. I'll see you in the morning.

All night I couldn't sleep. I just tossed and turned. This is the first fight we have had since we've been together and the first time I've slept without him. I couldn't help but silently cry. I don't know who's blowing this argument out of proportion, but I don't like it. I hate how he's making my feelings seem invalid in this situation.

I restlessly looked at the moon until tiredness took over me. I jumped up when I heard one of the bedroom doors close and Bully's big foot ass jogging down the stairs. I checked the time on my phone, and it was a little after 8 am. I got up to get dressed for my day. I couldn't wait to see my son. His little face will cheer me up for sure. I went into the bathroom to brush my teeth and wash my face. I felt a little hungover, but that wasn't going to stop me.

I picked out a simple but stylish outfit. I let my hair loose from my bonnet and touched up my weave. I didn't apply any makeup. Once I was dressed, I texted Erin letting her know I'd be there soon. Before I left, I went downstairs to grab a water bottle out of the kitchen. Bully was at the kitchen island eating a bowl of cereal. He looked at me like he wanted to say something but turned his head. He wanted to keep the problem going, so I made it easier for him and ignored his ass back. I grabbed my water and left. No bye or nothing. I got in my truck and headed straight to his mother's house.

When I got there, I parked in the driveway before knocking on the door. My mood instantly changed when she opened the door with KJ in her arms. I reached for him, and he smiled like he always does. I entered the house and pecked her on the cheek before sitting down.

"I felt like a part of me was missing all night," I said, kissing KJ all over his face.

"You're a mom now. You'll feel that frequently. Wait until you put him in daycare or send him to school. You'll cry ugly tears then." She giggled.

"So true. How did he do last night?"

"He did great. He didn't cry much and slept through one of his feedings. I'm sure he misses your touch."

"Awww. Thank you again for keeping him. I'm trying to open up to more nights." I giggled.

"I know it's rough in the beginning."

Before leaving, I strapped him in his car seat and grabbed his diaper bag. I couldn't wait to hurry up and get to Erin's house. I needed to vent, and I needed her to hear the whole story. It took me about twenty minutes to get to her house. I took KJ out of his car seat and grabbed his diaper bag. I knocked on the door, and Kiki opened it.

"Hi, auntie Keyshia. Can I hold him?" She asked.

"Go wash your hands first, Kiki." Mike came down the stairs and took my diaper bag and purse from me.

"Thank you," I told him.

I went into the living room to sit down. Kiki came and sat beside me, and I handed her KJ. She pecked his cheek, and he smiled. I loved to see the love she had for him. That's why I'll always have her back too.

"I'm trying to get all the love I can get before daddy takes me back to my mama's house."

"Aww. This weekend when you come back, you can come to my house and spend the day with me."

"Really?" She asked.

"I would love to hang out with you."

Kiki was such a sweet girl. She could spend the day with me whenever.

"Daddy, auntie Keyshia said I could stay with her when you pick me up this weekend. Could I go?" She asked when Mike came to hold KJ.

"Yes." He said, and she smiled.

"Can y'all be on your best behavior when I leave?" Mike said as Erin came down the stairs.

"Boy, leave and mind ya' business." She kissed him and gave Kiki a hug and a kiss.

"I'm serious." He looked at both of us and then left. I'm sure Bully gave him an ear full of lies.

"Let me wash my hands and get my baby." She walked into the kitchen. "Do you want to order Doordash for breakfast?"

"Yes, we can."

"Spill it."

"My heart is hurting so bad, friend," I admitted.

"Aww."

She took KJ out of my hands. She could see the pain in my face. We went back into the living room to talk while she ordered our breakfast for delivery.

"He cursed me out so bad last night. You know my crazy ass was arguing back, holding my ground too."

"But let me be real with you, friend. Y'all aren't dating anymore. You two are married with a child. No matter what, y'all are still a team. How do you guys avoid hating each other whenever there's a disagreement?" She asked.

"I don't know. I just snapped when he yelled at me. My problem wasn't even with the bitch anymore. It was with him."

"Well, what did he say?"

"He called me a hood rat!" She looked as confused as I did when he said it.

"Word for word, what did he say?"

"I have a child now and shouldn't be out here fighting like a hood rat."

"Bitch, that's what you're mad at?" She dropped her attitude.

"Wait, what?"

"That man doesn't want his wife fighting. That's why when you said he was sleeping in the other room, I was like, umm, why?"

"So I'm wrong?"

"Tell me the rest of the story."

I ran down everything that happened from when they left the club last night to when I left the house this morning. I expected her to be on my side, but it seems like she was leaning on Bully is right. I still don't see the problem.

"Listen, you just had a baby, and your emotions are still all over the place. That is very understandable. You haven't even gone to your six-week check-up yet, and you were molly whopping that bitch." She giggled. "He just wants you to be careful. I do agree that he shouldn't have yelled at you like that. You two were yelling at each other with your emotions on ten. Y'all both are passionate as fuck when you feel like you're right."

"I guess." I shrugged. I hate to admit that she was somewhat correct.

"Did you use a condom last night? Did he pull out? Did you take a Plan B?"

"No." I shook my head.

"Well, you are asking to have Irish twins."

"My mind wasn't even on that last night. When we got to the club, I felt free and like my old self before I had KJ. I'm struggling to find my identity of who I am now. It's a lot of pressure every day trying to be the best mom and wife, and I don't have Granny here to tell me what a wonderful job I'm doing. KJ needs me every second of the day, and I am in the house with him all day while Bully works. I'm wearing a smile on my face, but I'm losing my shit half the time." I sobbed.

"You may not think you are, but you might be going through Post-Partum Depression. That shit is very real, Keysh. That's why I try to help you as much as possible, so you have the support you need to heal."

"My hair has been falling out for the last couple of days. My body is going through so many changes it's ridiculous."

"You need to talk to your husband about this. You can't be petty with someone who doesn't know what's happening. He's working off a different type of emotion, and it's not fair for either of you."

"Don't get me wrong. He pulls his weight by ensuring he has KJ so I can rest, but it feels like our love life has died romantically. He asks more questions about KJ and his well-being than seeing if I just want to have an adult conversation. We talk about the baby all day. I'm dying for some of his romantic touches. That's why I felt like a princess last night because he wanted me again. He saw me as sexy and was attracted to me."

"It's the hormones, sis. Talk to your man."

"I'll try."

"First, we need to get you a Plan B. You don't want to find out you're pregnant at your next appointment."

"I'd die." I giggled.

She went upstairs to grab one out of her hoe stash. I took that shit immediately, praying it works until I can get on some type of birth control. Now she had my ass worried that I could potentially be pregnant. Lord, please be with my uterus.

Chapter 23

Erin Jackson

I've been trying to keep my mental health afloat since the grand opening of Mike's barbershop. I would lie if I said that seeing that boy show up and saying we were siblings didn't cut deep. It's a never ending cycle of trauma. I thought when Edward died, my past would stop trying to bite my ass but here goes another bug. I told everybody not to worry about it, but I needed to tell myself the same thing, but I couldn't. An hour ago, he found my Instagram page and sent me a message. I've been in deep thought since then.

I sipped my wine while I scrolled through his page. He had pictures with my mom, and they looked like the perfect family. She was smiling from ear to ear. I don't have any memories of her smiling. I just don't understand and could never see how this shit is okay. I picked up my phone to call Mike. I was home alone, and right now, I needed love around me.

"Wassup ma?" He answered.

"Hey, babe. When are you coming home?" I asked, biting my nails. My nerves were getting the best of me.

"I'm at the gas station. You okay?" He asked, hearing the tone of my voice.

"No, I'm not okay."

"Alright, I'm on my way home. You need me to bring you anything?"

"Just an ear to listen."

"Whatever it is, babe, I'm here."

"Thank you."

"You never have to thank me."

He hung up the phone, and I felt a little better knowing he'd be here. My phone buzzed with another message from that guy.

IsaacJackson21: ???

I ignored the message like the first one he sent. I don't know how to respond. While I waited for Mike to come home, I poured another glass of wine while I got the courage to talk about my feelings. Thankfully he didn't take a long time to come home. As soon as he entered, he rushed right to me.

"What happened, babe?"

"My mother's son found my Instagram and reached out to me."

"What he say?"

"Hi, Erin. I didn't mean to upset you or disrespect your place of business. I just wanted to meet with you and talk. I only found out about you recently and wanted answers. Mom doesn't want to speak about it, and I can't understand how she's so nonchalant about having another child. Please can you help me figure this out? Then he sent question marks thirty minutes ago because I didn't answer."

"She's still holding grudges twenty-something years later?" He asked.

"Evidently, she is. That woman is sick."

"I don't know what to tell you, babe. You can

answer and take this meeting as a way to end your issues with your mom and dad, or you can just ignore it and block him. I just don't want you to feel pressured into doing anything you're not ready for."

"I'm curious to know how I turned into a secret."

"This is some crazy shit." He shook his head.

"I agree."

I messaged him back finally and sent the address to a cafe in Los Angeles. I told him to be there in an hour and don't keep me waiting. I'm taking this shit back for myself. I haven't seen my mom since I was seven years old. She never had a change of heart and came to get me back. I have so much resentment towards her but also her family. My grandma acted like she cared about me and she never stepped in to do anything in my best interest. She watched her daughter toss her only granddaughter out like trash. I have no respect for any of them.

The only reason I'm agreeing to this is because Isaac has nothing to do with it. I rather my father gotten his useless ass wife pregnant than to impregnate me since there was a chance of that. I took a deep breath because I felt angry again, but I calmed down.

"Can you come with me?" I asked Mike.

"Of course, I can."

"Plus, I had a couple of glasses of wine. I need a responsible driver." I half smiled.

"I got you." He nodded his head.

I went upstairs to get dressed. I just needed to brush my teeth because I didn't want to smell like a drunk. I laid my hair down and sprayed on my perfume before slipping into my shoes and going to grab a bottle of water before leaving. I stayed quiet while Mike drove, and I smiled, seeing him stand as a soldier for me. He was always there by my side through all the trials and tribulations. I love this man. He's down to shoot it out for whatever.

"We're here." He parked in front of the cafe.

"Come on." I took a deep breath.

We got out of the truck and went inside. We sat by the door and waited. I told him to be here in an hour, which was fifty minutes ago. He has ten minutes to arrive, or I'm out the door. I wanted a pastry, so I ordered a muffin to calm my nerves. He took so long to come that I finished my muffin first.

"He's late, so let's go." I stood up to leave, but he entered the cafe at the same time.

"Hi, Erin." He said softly but still standing back.

I didn't say anything, but I sat down, and so did he. He looked afraid of Mike, and it made me giggle inside. At least someone knew not to mess with me because I had someone to protect me this time.

"Thank you for taking this meeting." He looked into my eyes. "Sorry for the commotion at your place of business." He said to Mike.

"You said you just found out about me?" I started the conversation.

"Yes. My grandma passed away two months ago, and in her obituary, it named you as one of her grandchildren. I was confused. Your picture was also in there." He took it out of his pocket and placed it in front of me.

That was indeed the grandmother I remember seeing as a child. The picture of me standing next to her with my father made my stomach turn in knots. I looked so scared. The picture was taken during the time my father was molesting me.

"You see the frown on my face in this picture?" Both Mike and Kyle nodded yes. "Your father was molesting me. I was terrified whenever that man was around. Look at how frightened I look, and I was so little."

Nobody had anything to say.

"He did?" He quizzed.

"Do you not believe me?"

"I never heard anything about why my father was sent to jail. Mama said he was wrongfully accused of something, but before he was able to prove his innocence, he was murdered."

"He was murdered for being a child molester. He wasn't in jail long before the inmates murdered him."

"I just want to know the truth, that's all. Can you tell me what happened to you?"

"Our father was abusive, and mama allowed it. She did whatever pleased him, and when she couldn't make him happy, he would come into my room at night while I screamed. It went on for a while before I told mama. She knew about it but did nothing to protect me. The way I was screaming in that house, there was no way the neighbors didn't hear. She didn't believe me when I told her what was happening. She called me out of my name so many times. That shit really hurt my feelings. I was only seven. So I told my teacher. I wasn't allowed to be released from school to my family that day. I went straight to a temporary placement with some Chinese people. I had to go to the hospital and get examined. The truth came out, but mama didn't want to believe it. She didn't even fight to bring me home since he was locked up and gone. She told CPS to take me and keep me. I haven't seen her since. That's the truth. She is still bitter to this day. She hates my guts and will see me catch on fire and not even piss on me to save me. I hope she gets the healing she deserves because she is one sick individual." I felt good to get that off of my chest.

"I'm so sorry that happened to you. I believe you. I knew something was always wrong with her. Growing up, I saw her lack of compassion and empathy. We are still working on our relationship. I am terribly sorry that happened to you."

He looked like he sympathized with me. Isaac and I seemed to be around the same height and had many of the same features. A blind person could tell we're related. He said he was turning twenty-two soon and just wanted to learn his identity after being lied to for so long. He is going to community college and is into gaming. I didn't care about any of it.

"Well, now that you have your answers do as you will." I got up so we could leave.

"Do you mind if we can keep in contact?" He asked.

"I do mind, actually. It took a lot for me to come here today. I came to tell my story and not let a bitter person write a false narrative for me. I don't want to speak of this again; unfortunately, you are linked to my trauma. You may not have done anything to me, but it hurts to see that man's face in yours."

He looked defeated, but I didn't care. Growing up, I didn't know how to say no; part of my healing is to say how I feel. It feels good to put my foot down. I don't want any communication from the past. Let's pray my dad doesn't dig himself up from the grave and find me.

Mike and I walked out of the cafe, and he opened the door for me to get in the truck. Once he got inside, he gave me a big hug, and I needed it. He heard my story before but not to this extent. To top it off, he saw a picture of me as a child in the worse moments of my life.

"I thought you were strong before today, but you are a courageous woman. I'm so proud of you, ma. That was nothing easy to do. I had chills listening to you, and nothing bothers me. I done murked plenty of niggas in my lifetime, but this was some brave shit."

"That's a nice compliment." I giggled.

"For real, you need to write a book and tell your story or something."

"That might be a great idea, actually." I might take him up on that. I could see myself now helping the voiceless people.

"Whatever you want for dinner, let's go get it. You deserve a great meal."

"Can we order our food and sit on the beach? I just want to be by the water right now."

"Anything, ma."

He drove toward the beach, and we found a restaurant nearby to order from. We settled on some fancy pizza. It was only 6 pm, and I'm glad it wasn't dark. I wanted to be able to see the water clearly. After getting our food and drinks, we walked to the beach and sat comfortably in front of the water. It was a little cold, but we both had on a jacket. I loved that he didn't care he was wearing his twenty-five hundred dollar Dior shoes in the sand. He just wanted to live in the moment with me.

"This pizza is good as hell." He tore it up, and I giggled.

"I'm ready to try and have a child." It was something on my mind since I met Isaac.

"Are you serious?" He put the pizza down.

"You are an incredible man and father already. There's no better guy than you, honestly. I'm ready to heal the hurt little girl in me. I always wondered what it would be like to have parents who cared about my well-being. Now my child will have two parents who love them to the moon and back."

"We can start right now." He leaned over to kiss me.

"I'm serious. I'll throw my birth control in the trash, and we'll see how long it takes before I get pregnant."

"I'm happy you changed your mind."

"I am too. This was the last piece to my healing."

We sat and ate our food while we talked. Our life is heading in the right direction. We just bought a house, are newly engaged, and planning for a child of our own. I'm excited about this. We deserve to be happy together. Our relationship has been about healing me, and it's time to turn the fuck up now 'cause I'm good.

Chapter 24

Khalil "Bully" Wright

Keyshia had her six-week check-up appointment today, but when she came back home, she didn't say shit to me. I get that we are beefing right now, but the least she could do is let me know how her health is. This shit has blown so out of proportion that we are not telling each other the important shit. She doesn't wanna speak to me, and when she does, it's a few words about KJ.

"You really not gonna let me know what your doctor said about your health?" I was hot right now.

"Leave me alone, Khalil."

She strapped KJ in his car seat before I picked him up and took him to the car. We were heading to a family photoshoot that my mom put together. Now that KJ is here, she wanted updated family photos. Keyshia had an attitude toward me, but she was secretly excited about the pictures. She was into this hopeless romantic shit.

Neither of us spoke while I drove, but when we got to the photo studio, she put on her fake smile and pretended we were cool. My girl is really fake, and that's something I didn't know that in the beginning about her.

"Y'all two still bickering?" My mom said that when

I tried to help Keyshia change KJ into his matching outfit, she rejected my help.

"No." She lied.

"Stevie Wonder could see the division between you two. Get y'all shit together and put a real smile on your face for these pictures. Don't come up in here ruining my damn pictures. I'm taking my grandson tonight, and y'all two go work this shit out. Got everybody in here walking on eggshells because y'all are avoiding your problems." My mom didn't usually get out of character, but I could tell she was mad as fuck. Keyshia didn't take offense to it because she knew my mom was talking to her like a mother.

"Yes, ma'am." We said together.

"Come outside for a minute." I pulled her by her arm.

We stood outside for privacy. I leaned against the wall, trying to collect my thoughts. She had been extra sensitive lately, so I don't want her feeling attacked again. She was acting childish, and I wanted her to see my point.

"What are we doing?" I held her hand so she could see I wasn't being combative with her.

"I don't know." She sounded like she wanted to cry.

"Can I take you to dinner so we can talk this out the correct way?" I looked into her eyes.

"Yes, please."

"Please don't cry. Your makeup looks good. We gonna fix it." I hugged her and kissed her on her forehead before walking back inside.

I hate how everybody else felt uncomfortable because we were at odds. We all checked that our outfits were put together before we started to take the pictures. We wore all white even KJ. Surprisingly he didn't fuss throughout the pictures. He stayed chill and even smiled for some photos. My mom wanted group photos, pictures of her and just KJ, pictures of her and Keyshia, and some with just her boys.

When we were done, I helped my mom put KJ in her car. She had everything KJ needed at her house, including clean clothes, his bassinet, and all the diapers and formula. She was an amazing grandmother, and she was over prepared for him. This is something she always wanted, so I expected this from her.

"Y'all come kiss y'all baby so that we can go home." She was upset with Keyshia and me.

We did as she said because we didn't want to upset her further.

"Y'all both are going to come to pick him up together tomorrow. Don't let whatever it is ruin the foundation y'all built. Get it together y'all." She hugged us both, and we watched her drive off.

"She told us, didn't she?" Keyshia shook her head.

"Where do you want to eat?" I asked.

"Let me see who has open reservations." She pulled out her phone. "Ruth's Chris has a table in an hour."

"We'll make it there in time with this traffic."

I opened the truck door and helped her get in. I wanted to start the conversation now, so it would be in the car with privacy if anything escalated. I didn't want her crying in the restaurant. Sometimes she didn't know how to act when being called out for her shit.

"I want to put an end to this fighting. These last couple of days have been rough, but the icing on the cake is if we're beefing, that's cool, but when it comes to our health, safety, and son, you stop the bullshit. I'm not your enemy, babe."

"My feelings are hurt, Khalil. I can't deny that. How you looked at me and yelled at me in the heat of that fight fucked with me. It's one thing to put me in my place in private but to do that in front of so many people bothered me. We are a team, and you picked your side when you came down to the bar that night."

"In the midst of you doing all that fighting and still trying to swing on her when we broke it up, you didn't hear me talking to you nicely, right? You only heard me when I yelled at you?"

"Yes."

"I apologize for yelling at you. You know I don't talk to you like that. When I tried to break it up, you wanted blood, so you weren't hearing shit I had to say. The only time you listened to me was when I yelled. I said numerous times to break it up. You were fucking possessed."

"I saw her and snapped. She said I had no right to kick her out of the club. I already took her man, and that's when I jumped on her."

"It bothers me that you allow shit like that to happen. I'm a good ass man to you. I never once lied to you or made you question my sincerity, so why are you letting weird bitches get in your head? You know who your man is. You know who put that ring on your finger, so act like it. If you didn't want her in the club, act like the boss you are and have one of the security escort her ass out. Whatever you say goes, and you know that. You are a mom now. You ain't supposed to be fighting."

"I understand that." She murmured.

"Don't ever tell me I picked a side. I'm on your side always. It's only one side to be on, and you know that."

"I'm sorry."

"Talk to me. I don't want one word replies. How do you feel?"

"Erin already checked me about me acting like a brat, but I had to keep my attitude since you kept yours. Look, babe, I am sorry. It's no excuse for my actions. I'm honestly going through something, though."

"What are you going through?" I needed to know because this is my first time hearing this.

"Post-partum depression. I don't feel like myself. I don't know who this woman is, and I don't know how to navigate this new me. I feel so lost. I love you and KJ, but I don't love myself right now. I have always been confident and secure, but I can't recognize this woman. I talked to my doctor about it, and she said my hormones are still all over the place. I have to try my best to take some time for myself while I care for everybody else. My feelings get hurt when I see you come, and you're just excited to see KJ. I want a kiss too. I wish you would ask how my day was and have small talk. I miss our intimacy when I felt like the only person in your world."

"I didn't know I made you feel like that, babe. I'm just excited as fuck to be a father and didn't have the intention to make you feel unloved. You have my attention now, and I promise I'll do better. One day out of the week, let's save it for us to have a date. Just you and I and my mama could spend the day with KJ."

"I would like that."

"Plus, you been looking sexy as fuck. Your body got thicker, and your ass jiggles more. I don't know what you see in the mirror, but my baby mama is fine as fuck." I was dead serious too.

"Thank you." She giggled.

I parked the truck when we pulled up to the

restaurant. We held hands and walked inside. Thankfully we were able to be seated right away. It was a week and a half of us not speaking, so we had a lot to tell each other. I'm just happy we're good again. The house was miserable as fuck. I missed seeing the smile on her face. She's too beautiful to be mad all the time. Now that I know what's been happening with her, I'll handle her more carefully.

The next afternoon I met up with Mike at the barbershop. We've been so busy working and making plays that we didn't hang out unless it was with Keyshia and Erin. We saw each other almost every day, but it was always on business.

"This place stays packed," I said as he opened a shampoo box in the back room.

"This place is gold." He chuckled. "You and wifey good now?" He asked.

"I had to put it down on her. You know what I mean?" I joked. "Nah, but seriously we are good. She said her hormones are still all over the place after having KJ."

"That shit is real nigga. You remember how Shana was after she had Kiki? That bitch was crazy." We both couldn't stop laughing.

"I'm trying to be on her good side. Those couple of days were like living in hell."

"I feel you. What you gonna do about the broad?"

"I'ma unblock her number and put it on speaker so Keyshia could hear. I don't need none of that bickering about me contacting her. That bitch is annoying as fuck."

"Be careful with that one. You got a problem I don't

want." I waved him off.

"I'ma head out. I'm tryna come home earlier so she could have a break to herself."

"Alright, be safe. I'ma come by later and see my nephew. Kiki has been bugging me."

"Come through," I said before leaving.

I left out of the barbershop and headed to a nearby flower shop to pick something up for my girl. I wanted her to see how dedicated I am to making her mental health a priority of mine. I needed her to be good, so we could focus on making the next baby. I needed a daughter next.

I picked up a rose in a box shaped like a heart. I know she would love it. That shit was expensive too. I also got a box of chocolates. I paid for everything and left. I couldn't wait to get home so she could see the smile on her face. I made it home in twenty minutes. I parked in the garage and hopped out quickly. KJ was in his baby swing while she made dinner.

"What you making?" I could smell the food from the garage. "These are for you." I handed her the gifts.

"Aww, baby, thank you." She pecked my lips. "I'm making spaghetti and a salad. Are you ready to eat?"

"I'm starving."

"Okay, I'll make your plate."

I washed my hands before taking KJ out of his swing. I kissed my twin before taking him to sit with me while Keyshia made my plate. I checked the time, and it was time for his feeding.

"It's time for him to eat, right?" I asked to make sure.

"Yes, I'll make his bottle in a second."

"It's okay, babe. I got it. You can eat your food first

and breathe. I'll feed him and burp him." She smiled and went back to making our plates.

I rather my son eat first anyways. I could wait twenty minutes. I'm sure she barely ate today, so she needed to eat. I made his six-ounce bottle and watched him guzzle it down without stopping to breathe. When he was done, I patted his back to make him burp. He was chunky and seemed like he couldn't wait to dig into our plates.

"How was your day?" I asked her.

"It was good we walked around the neighborhood, and I was able to get some laundry done."

"What did you do for yourself today?"

"I'm about to go shower and spray on my favorite perfume. Then maybe we can watch a movie together?"

"If that's what you want to do, we can."

"I do." She smiled.

I smiled back. Her love and smile are intoxicating. If she's happy, then I am too. That's all I wanted for her. KJ rested in my arms while I ate my dinner. Keyshia went to take her shower and get her mind together. I couldn't wait to chill with her too. I enjoyed coming home, and it was just us three. I always wanted this.

Chapter 25

Epilogue

Erin Simmons

I added my signature to the last book before taking a picture with one of my readers. My book signing was coming to an end at Barnes and Nobles. I have been on a book tour for the last month, meeting many broken souls ready to heal. Mike suggested I write a book about my life two years ago, and I took his advice. At first, it helped me to vent on paper, but it was the healing many people needed. So I decided to publish it.

"Thank you so much for coming." I hugged the lady before she walked away.

I looked to my side and smiled, seeing my handsome husband lean on the bookshelves holding our son Mason. It has been two years since we have been married, and soon after, I got pregnant with our first child together. Mason is the perfect mix of Mike and me. He is turning one soon, and I couldn't wait to celebrate his incredible life.

"Can you sign my book?" Mike held up a hard copy of my book *Healing Begins With You.*

"For you sure! What's your name?" I played along with him.

"Michael."

"To Michael, the handsome, tall chocolate man I gave my heart to, I love you to the moon and back. I don't know how I would navigate life without you. Thank you for helping me want better for myself. Love your fly ass wife." I giggled.

"Now that's how do you it." He chuckled before leaning in to place a kiss on my lips.

"Where did Kiki go?" I asked, worried that she had wandered off.

"Keyshia and Bully took her to buy more books." I shook my head and giggled.

Kiki is my mini-me for sure. When I started to write my book, she turned into a bookworm. She loved reading and thought it was so cool I was writing a book. She says she hopes to write a book one day, too, and I'll push her in the right direction when she's ready.

"You did amazing!" Keyshia ran up to hug me when they returned.

"Thank you. I missed you guys so much."

"You have been gone for a month too long!" We hugged tightly.

I bent down to hug my nephew KJ and my niece Camille. Keyshia and I were two months apart when I had Mason. Now she is pregnant with their third child. Bully kept her trapped in the house and was using her to breed his babies because this girl could not have a pregnant free summer to save her life.

"I'm home now. What are we doing?" I asked.

"I have a bottle of Ace for you to celebrate at my house. I'll have food delivery in under an hour."

"That sounds good! I just want to relax and enjoy my family."

I sold out of all my books. I didn't have much to pack, just my banners and special pens. Mike helped, and I was done in five minutes. We left The Grove and headed to Keyshia and Bully's house. Mike had to stop at the gas station first for blunts and gas. I leaned the seat back and relaxed. It felt good to be home. I missed spending quality time with my family. For the last month, it has been all work. I needed a break to relax and decompress. My publisher is already working on my second book tour. I don't know how I'll keep up.

Keyshia Wright

I had Mike stall for extra time. He threw her a big welcome home party at our house. I am sure she didn't suspect a thing. When I arrived home, I made sure everything was in place. All our friends and family were here to support and show her love.

"Where do you want these balloons?" Bully asked.

"Put it in the foyer, please." I scrubbed KJ's face. He had an Oreo, and the aftermath on his face and hands was terrible.

I had Jasmine here, making sure the setup was top tier. We had a whole buffet of food and drinks to last for weeks. Mike just wanted it to be a good vibe for her. He texted me, telling me he was pulling up. We all ran outside, waiting for them to pull up. So many cars were in the driveway, so we decided to bring the surprise outside. When his truck pulled in, Erin got out of the car laughing. She was so happy and shocked. I don't know how she thought we wouldn't celebrate this big win for her.

"No, you guys didn't." Tears ran down her face.

"You deserve it!" I shouted.

Mike escorted her into the house, and Bully grabbed Mason and Kiki out of the truck. Inside we celebrated for hours. The men were outside playing an aggressive game of dominos while my ratchet ass twerked to the music.

"That's why yo' ass is about to have three kids under three," Kaylen said.

"You don't have to hurt my feelings like that." I laughed because why are you telling my business like that?

"Are you done having kids after you give birth to Nova?" Bre asked.

"Bully wants another boy. So hopefully, baby number four is a boy so that I can close these legs."

"Nothing about them legs are ever closed." Jasmine joked, and we all laughed.

I was five months pregnant and have gotten used to being pregnant after so many times. I went from one kid to three in a blink of an eye. Bully and I both wanted to expand our family, and we will not be sorry for having as many kids as we want. Speaking of Bully, we are on cloud nine in our marriage. I had a lot of maturing to do, and I was reminded of that. I loved my man like no other, but that didn't give me a reason to be childish sometimes. When I didn't get my way, I was ready to break everything and throw the whole marriage away, but I had to get smacked with reality. Of course, marriage is hard as fuck, but I want war behind that man.

Bre and Logic's daughter Leah started crying. Bre gave birth to her two months ago, so it's expected for her to fuss when she's hungry or tired. Her mama made her a bottle. I still couldn't believe Logic is a father now. He's still immature, but not like how he used to be. That boy will never take anything seriously, but that's just his sense of humor. He makes Leah laugh all day because he's so funny. Since she's been born, she has changed his life for the better. He and Bre are still going strong. She is just as crazy as my ass. I can't wait to see what the future has in store for them. I love his growth. Hopefully, Bully and Mike see it, too, so he can take over the family business one day.

When all of us met in the beginning, we had nothing. It's crazy to see how all of our lives changed for the better in four years. I'm glad I met my man when I did. I now have family, and the pain of not having my mom and Granny alive hurts a lot less these days. I know they're proud of me.

The End